ENTER
AT YOUR OWN
RISK

ANIRBAN BHATTACHARYYA

FiNGERPRINT!

Published by
FiNGERPRINT!
An imprint of Prakash Books India Pvt. Ltd

113/A, Darya Ganj,
New Delhi-110 002
Email: info@prakashbooks.com/sales@prakashbooks.com

 Fingerprint Publishing
 @FingerprintP
 @fingerprintpublishingbooks
www.fingerprintpublishing.com

ISBN: 978 93 6214 843 8

To my wife Erum,
who does not get scared
at horror movies or stories.

CONTENTS

PREFACE

How many times have you heard about a particular place being haunted? Or a locality which has a paranormal presence? Or stories and legends that creep you out about an old fort, an abandoned village, or even just a forest?

Are the stories true, or are they mere myths and urban legends that have gathered credence over the years through oral retellings—each generation adding their inputs?

Here is a book inspired by the scariest and the paranormal urban legends associated with some very well-known haunted places across India. A modern meta-fiction. Each story takes us into the world of these haunted places with its history, and the urban legends and marries it with a modern-day fiction narrative. What happens when the two worlds collide—the story of the place and our characters?

What is a spooky story without the right ambience, correct? For the first time in the world—here is a book that comes with its own background music! To enhance your reading experience, I have inserted QR codes in the stories. When you scan the codes you will get an exclusive background music for the particular 'scene' that you will be reading. Hopefully you will feel like you are in the middle of a movie, as it will transport you right into the world of the stories!

From the Producer and Writer of *Fear Files*, the Creator, Producer, Writer & Director of *Savdhaan India*, and the Producer of *Crime Patrol*, comes this spooky offering.

ACKNOWLEDGMENT

I t took me quite a while to write this book; more than it should have, having to stop writing at 3 a.m. or 4 a.m. as I got spooked by my own writing or when I could sense someone standing in the room—or maybe it was just my imagination. Having grown up in a boarding school in Kalimpong, I spent many sleepless nights hearing the cottage creak at night which scared the hell out of me!

But here we are.

Firstly, I want to thank my literary agent, Suhail Mathur and The Book Bakers, for our sixth collaboration! Your support helps me take these stories from across genres to the world. Suhail, thank you!

Next, the amazing and brilliant team at Fingerprint, Prakash Books who make me feel like the best writer in the world! The team led by Executive Publisher, Shantanu Duttagupta, ably supported by Sarita Prasad and Sampurna Kundu of Marketing and Promotions, Gavin Morris who creates mind-blowing artwork and covers, and editor Shilpa Mohan. Let's create history again as we did with *The Hills Are Burning*.

To my late grandmother, Kamala Devi Bhattacharyya, who instilled in me the love for stories and writing. Every night she narrated a bedtime story—and transported me to many new worlds.

To my wife Erum and son Kabir—*'Ab yeh wala toh padh lo!'* You are incredible and you allow me to be selfish and chase my dream, book after book . . . I am so grateful and blessed!

To 'Doc' Siddharth Nirwan—thanks for the amazing trip to Bhangarh; and to his wife Mahima Panwar, sons Archie and Richie—you guys are amazing!

Thanks to Meg Young who introduced me to the descendant of the Abbott family—Quinton Rochfort who shed light on the 'real' story and life of John Abbott.

Thank you Amrish Sethi for being so kind and patiently proofreading the manuscript and giving valuable inputs, as always!

To my friends and family who have now started dreading me writing another book as they will need to buy it—I have a dozen and more books to write. You are not getting away easy. Jokes aside, thank you for your encouragement and belief, always.

And to my readers who have shown so much love and support even though I have written across genres. You have jumped with me with every book, willing to hold my hand as we traveled together. Here is one more leap of faith.

Get to know me at www.linktr.ee/anirbanb

BHANGARH

Bhangarh is a village situated in Rajgarh, Alwar, Rajasthan, at the edge of the Sariska Tiger Reserve. It is famous for its historical ruins. But what makes it more attractive is its reputation of being one of the most haunted places of India.

It was established in 1573 during the rule of Kachwaha Rajput ruler of Jaipur Bhagwant Das as the residence of his second son Madho Singh, the younger brother of Emperor Akbar's general, Man Singh I. After Madho Singh's death, the next ruler of Bhangarh was his son, Chhatra Singh, after whose death in 1630, Bhangarh slowly declined.

There are many theories about the end of Bhangarh.

One of them is that in 1783, there was a great famine, after which Bhangarh was deserted. This, of course, is the most boring one.

The second is about a beautiful princess Ratnavati who displeased a tantric, who before dying, cursed the city.

The third is about a sadhu, Guru Balu Nath, who lived on the hill on which Raja Bhagwant Singh built the fort. The sadhu's only condition was that the shadow of the fort should never cast a shadow on his own humble dwelling. Ajab Singh, when he was a ruler, defied this and built columns, whose shadows fell on the sadhu's house. The sadhu then cursed the fort to ruin, as well as the city. To this day, a small stone hut, known as tantric ki *chhatri* overlooks the fort.

Trespassing near Bhangarh is legally prohibited between sunset and sunrise. A signboard posted by the Archeological Survey of India on the site states:

"Entering the borders of Bhangarh before sunrise and after sunset is strictly prohibited. Legal action will be taken against anybody who does not follow these instructions".

But two people defied this rule, and the legends of Bhangarh . . .

THE
HAUNTED VILLAGE

"Are you sure about doing this?" Chinmay asked as he settled into his bed and pulled the duvet over himself. It was cold. Rajasthan in December meant that winter was slowly sweeping in like a blanket over the region; and room heaters would make their presence felt.

"Why? Are you having second thoughts?" Nisha asked with one eyebrow raised.

It was a guesthouse built in the style of a traditional Rajasthani haveli. At least the windows, the corridors, the pillars, and the courtyard all seemed to be that of an ancient haveli. It felt almost like a movie set. Dressed up for the occasion but empty inside. The receptionist Munawar had assured them that the house once belonged to a landlord who had dealings with the Rajasthani royalty. In fact, he had pointed out a few ancient black-and-white photographs trapped inside gilded frames, which showed a man in his late fifties in various modes of activity.

In one, he had his right foot on top of a tiger that had met its fate at the hands of the man whose foot now rested on it. In another, he was seated on a throne-like chair with his mustache waxed and erect. In another, the man—wait a minute—was a completely different man! The only similar thing was the mustache.

"You know they could have bought these photographs from a *chor-bazaar* or collected them from various houses!" Nisha said in a hushed tone, trying to keep her voice as low as possible so that her doubts would not reach Munawar's ears.

"Who cares? We got an awesome deal, we saved money, and meals are included!" Chinmay said.

"Get out of bed! We have to be there for dinner, remember?" Nisha nudged Chinmay, and when that didn't work, she pulled the duvet off him.

"Nishu! You are worse than Mom! She at least gives me ten extra minutes in bed!" Chinmay made a face of mock sadness.

"Yes, she has spoilt you, and is not here to bring you your dinner, saying—Chinu, *ye lo* dinner!" Nisha imitated Chinmay's mom as she playfully pretended to bring in an imaginary tray of imaginary food.

Chinmay lunged and pulled Nisha onto the bed. She fell on him. They were inches apart. He could smell her sweet breath. He came forward to kiss her. Just then, a knock interrupted their sweet reverie.

Nisha rolled her eyes, left the bed, and opened the door of their hotel room.

"Madam, dinner is being served. And the evening entertainment show will begin," one of the room-service men, dressed in traditional Rajasthani attire of dhoti and angarkha, complete with the headdress, stood at their door. His mustache, though, suffered from erectile dysfunction.

"We will be there," Nisha assured him, and she shut the door.

The arrangement was nice. A warm bonfire was at the center of the quadrangle, surrounded by the hotel guests and a buffet table in the corner. The show had already begun. Women were performing the Ghoomar dance, while the foreigners were going berserk trying to click pictures and soak in the sight and sound. Chinmay and Nisha chose a cozy corner to sit in.

"So where are you from?" a voice piped in. Chinmay looked to see the source of the voice and discovered that it belonged to a Caucasian man, aged about 65.

"From Delhi," Chinmay replied, "And what about you?"

"Dunfermline," the man replied.

"Where's that?" Nisha asked.

"Scotland," the man said in his slightly Scottish accent.

"First time to India?" Nisha asked.

"No, I lived in Goa back in the 80's in Arambol. But left. I keep coming back . . . but this probably will be my last." There was sadness in his voice, "By the way I am Christopher. You can call me Chris."

"That's Nisha and I am Chinmay. Why did you say last visit?"

Chris thought for a bit. "I have the big C. Just another few months before my lease runs out!" And he burst into a guffaw.

"Oh I am so sorry!" Chinmay apologized.

"Oh don't be silly! Your first time in Rajasthan?" Chris changed the topic.

"Yes!" Nisha said—glad that the pall of gloom had risen. "We drove up from Delhi this evening, and tomorrow evening we head to Bhangarh."

"Say again?" The expression on Chris' face suddenly darkened, "Bhangarh? The haunted village?"

Chinmay nodded.

"Are you guys nuts?" Chris hissed trying to keep his voice down.

"Do you even know how dangerous it is?" Chris asked.

"It's all make-believe, mumbo-jumbo!" Nisha said.

Chris' white face was now crimson—like the color of the wine that they were sipping on—"I have been there . . . like you, as a joke . . . I know! That place is evil!"

He now had Chinmay and Nisha's attention.

"He will be there . . . He is always there!" Chris' voice had now dipped into a hoarse whisper!

"Who?" Nisha asked, intrigued and nervous.

"The priest who cursed the village! His spirit roams the streets of Bhangarh!"

"We don't believe in ghosts or spirits!" Nisha dismissed Chris with one sweeping remark.

"Then why do you think it is shut after dark?" Why?" Chris' face turned into a grimace, trying to drive home reason.

Before Nisha or Chinmay could say anything, Chris walked away—"Get some sleep, kids! This is not some Halloween trick-or-treat. I am going back to my room. Goodnight!"

They stared at Chris, who walked away down the hotel corridor and disappeared around a corner.

"What was wrong with him?" Nisha snuggled into bed.

"Well, every one of our friends back at the office had warned us as well, right?" Chinmay was absorbed in his phone, busy answering his WhatsApp messages

"So are you scared now?"

Chinmay kept his phone aside and pulled Nisha so that she was just inches away. The cold winter night formed goose bumps on her arm, as he slowly traced a finger down it.

"Well, I don't have a choice, do I? Wherever this hot woman goes, I have to follow like a knight in shining armor to protect you," his voice dipped and became a breathy hoarse whisper, "see that no one gets to touch or harm you!"

With this Chinmay came forward and met her lips. Nisha put her hand behind his head and pulled him in. She could taste the wine on his lips, and the inside of his mouth, as her tongue met his, in a passionate and somewhat inebriated embrace.

He gently lowered her down on the bed, and slowly slid the spaghetti strap of her camisole off her shoulder. Chinmay buried his face in the crook of her neck and kissed her.

Nisha arched her back and gasped. He always knew where to touch her. She hurriedly took his shirt off. And as they wrestled beneath the sheets in a race against time to lose their clothes, they kept coming back to touch, caress, kiss, and nuzzle.

"If something does happen to us tomorrow, let's make love like it is the last time," Nisha said and giggled.

It was a funny thing to say when in the throes of making love.

Nisha slowly slid herself out from beneath Chinmay and pushed him onto the bed, and then mounted him. He could feel himself slowly slip into the comforting warmth that he knew and longed for. Chinmay gasped. Something was different.

He had never been so aroused. When it was over, she collapsed on Chinmay's chest. Their bodies were covered in sweat despite the winter cold.

Nisha soon fell asleep, guided by the rhythmic heaving of Chinmay's chest, like the swinging of a baby's cot. Chinmay stayed awake for a while, caressing her hair, and a hundred thoughts racing through his head. He didn't know when he fell asleep.

At breakfast, they kept a lookout for Chris. They wanted to get to know more about the place from him. But he was nowhere to be seen. Chinmay asked one of the waiters about Chris, but the latter didn't know.

Nisha went and asked the manager of the hotel about which room was Chris checked into . . .

"You know, he was from Scotland; he was tall, blonde, aged about, early 60s . . . he was with us at the dinner program," Nisha tried her best to profile Chris.

"Sorry ma'am—we have no guests matching that description," the manager replied, and then continuing, "Maybe he was a walk-in guest from some other hotel."

"It can't be. He said he was going back to his room, when he left us. And he headed down the corridor," Chinmay argued.

There was no sign of Chris. Nobody knew him. Nobody had seen him.

It was still cold when they stepped out of the hotel, the next afternoon. Raghu was waiting for them with the car. For an extra buck tourist guides were willing to flout the rules laid down by the Government of not entering Bhangarh after sunset.

"It's 3.30 p.m. now. It will take us two hours to drive there. We should be there before sunset," Raghu opened the door of the car to allow Nisha to get in. Chinmay and Nisha were both carrying small backpacks. They had stuffed it with Maglite torches, water bottles, a few snacks, and night vision glasses.

"I am going to drop you off at the entrance. And then tomorrow morning at 5.00 a.m. I'll come back to pick you up. You are not going to get any mobile signals, so you have to stick to each other," Raghu was maneuvering the car through the city traffic.

"So which story is the true story about what happened at Bhangarh?" Nisha asked.

"The story about Emperor Madho Singh and the sadhu is what people mostly believe in. Emperor Madho Singh took permission from the sadhu Balu Nath to build the township. The sadhu had only one condition—that the shadow of the Palace should not fall on the sadhu's house," Raghu narrated the memorized and oft-repeated tale.

"But it did," Chinmay cut in.

"Yes and the curse of the sadhu came true—Bhangarh turned into a city of ruins, and no structure could survive, how much they ever tried to rebuild," Raghu smiled, "And people believe this story to be true as the tomb of Guru Balu Nath still stands in Bhangarh."

Nisha shivered as a chill went up her spine.

"You okay?" Chinmay asked. Nisha nodded.

It was 5.15 p.m. when they reached the Hanuman Gate of Bhangarh—named so, after the Hanuman temple located there. They walked past the Ticket Counter.

"You wait here," Raghu said as he walked toward an approaching elderly man. They watched as Raghu and the old man chatted, and then shook hands as money was transferred from one palm to the other.

"It's done. You can go in—but remember if you feel uneasy—head toward Hanuman Gate and exit Bhangarh," Raghu, it seemed, was suddenly in a hurry to leave.

"Do you believe that Bhangarh is haunted?" Nisha asked.

Without missing a beat, Raghu replied, "Yes . . . some parts more than others. Stay as far away from the Palace and Modon ki Haveli. I'll be staying half an hour from here. So if you do get out of the ruins during the night, then head to the lamp post there," Raghu said as he pointed to a derelict lamp post about 100 meters from the parking lot, "you can get mobile network from that spot. Call me and I'll come and pick you up. Now go before the sun sets." And with that Raghu got into his car and drove off.

They walked into the village of Bhangarh through Hanuman Gate. Immediately the temperature seemed to drop. On the right was an old tree smeared with vermillion and at the base of which lay flowers. And beside it was a white structure—the Hanuman Temple.

"Pray for protection so that you can see daylight tomorrow," the guard's tone had an eerie chill to it.

"We don't believe in ghosts and spirits," Chinmay dismissively thwarted any preconceived notion that the guard may have about them being scared.

The guard laughed, which echoed in his chest with a series of deep wheezes. Hocking a mouthful of phlegm on to the ground, the guard spoke again—"By the time the night is over, you will become a believer!"

With that, the guard walked off.

They walked into the village step by step, their adrenaline slowly building up. They had planned to do this a year ago;

and now that they were walking on Bhangarh's very soil, the excitement was slowly sinking into them.

They were standing in front of an orange map etched in stone, which showed the layout of the ancient village.

"You ready to do this?" Chinmay looked to Nisha, who seemed to be hypnotized.

"Huh? Yes! I just can't believe we are finally here!" Nisha's voice seemed to quiver. Chinmay wondered whether it was excitement or nervousness.

He clicked a picture of the map on his cell phone.

A light breeze was blowing through, that further dipped the temperature. There was an eerie stillness that was sharp and cold. Their footsteps echoed as they walked on the stone-laden streets. Even the sound of their breathing seemed to get magnified and it played back inside their heads like the sound in an empty auditorium. There were ruins on both sides of the path.

"Just imagine this place was once a thriving . . ." before Chinmay could finish his sentence . . .

Suddenly a sharp shriek ripped through the silence. A fast-fleeting shadow darted across the road and took refuge behind one of the stone walls. Chinmay jumped.

"Fuck!" Chinmay yelled and fell down.

They looked toward the source of movement.

"Did you see that?" Chinmay's voice struggled to emerge from his suddenly parched throat. The evening sun was fast retreating into the shadows.

Nisha was rooted to the ground—staring at the ruins of the wall.

Suddenly, a human-like hand appeared from behind and gripped onto the wall. Nisha and Chinmay held their breath, retreating with tiny steps. A black figure leaped out suddenly and shrieked. Chinmay and Nisha trying to walk and run backward fell onto their backpacks and shrieked. A monkey was staring at them inquisitively, with its head cocked to one side.

Chinmay had stopped breathing and had grown red in the face. He started laughing, at first nervously, and then in loud guffaws! Chinmay helped Nisha up. The monkey seemed used to human presence, probably because of the tourists that thronged Bhangarh during the day. Chinmay picked up a loose stone from the ground and threw it at the monkey. The stone smacked the monkey on the side of its face; and it scampered off, squealing.

"You didn't need to do that!" Nisha hit Chinmay on his back playfully.

"Serves the bastard right for scaring us like that."

They walked toward a large structure. The light was fading fast. The sky was blood red. The light cast a hue on the structure. With each step, the structure appeared to be towering menacingly over them. It was a two-storeyed structure with its front completely ripped out and destroyed, exposing its innards for the world to see. There was something very creepy about this building. Most of it was now covered in patches of darkness. Chinmay put on his Maglite and pointed it at the ruined haveli.

"What is this structure?" Nisha asked, "It's giving me the creeps!"

Chinmay checked the picture of the map on his phone and then said, "This is Modon ki Haveli."

They looked at each other. They knew to whom the house belonged, once upon a time when this village was abuzz and alive. They had read about him, when they had researched about Bhangarh.

Modon was a ruthless merchant who traded in gold and precious stones. He had several shops in the Jauhari Bazaar, a five-minute walk from his haveli. But beneath the innocent demeanor of the tradesman lurked the most heinous devil. It was said that he had an appetite for young girls. And when he was satiated with them, the girls were never to be seen. Buried in the catacombs deep under the haveli, the victims became a part of the foundation.

A screech rent through the air. The hair on the back of Chinmay's neck stood up. He turned around and pointed his torch in every direction he could. Nisha's breathing was loud and quick paced.

"Must be an owl," Chinmay pacified Nisha.

Just then, they distinctly heard a giggle. A young girl's giggle gently wafting through the silence. They pointed their torch at the haveli. The light lit up the destroyed arches of the first floor.

"Chinu, let's move . . . please let's walk ahead," Nisha caught hold of Chinmay's hand and forced him to move. Chinmay noticed that Nisha's hand was clammy and cold.

"We could turn around and just get out of here, you know."

"We've planned this for so long. Maybe just spend another half hour and then we could head out and call Raghu," Nisha said.

It was pitch black now. The sky was beautifully laid out like a tapestry of shining lights. They looked up.

"Wow! I haven't seen such a clear sky in a long, long time!" Chinmay said, gulping some water.

They walked.

The air seemed to get heavier and heavier—its weight pushing down on the two of them.

"I wish there was some breeze . . . it is getting so stifling," Nisha complained, taking off her jacket, and immediately felt cold and started putting it back on. "What is wrong with the weather?"

They walked past some ruins of what were homes and houses.

"This is so weird!" Chinmay said as he stood outside one of the ruined houses.

"What is?" Nisha said as she zipped up her jacket.

"The houses. They were all double-storey houses. But they all look like they have been neatly sliced in half . . . like a hot knife has just gone through butter and exposed the mid-section!" Chinmay stood and adjusted his backpack.

"And when you think it was a curse that did this, it makes it more eerie and supernatural!" Nisha had walked ahead and as Chinmay walked to catch up with her—they realized that they now stood in front of a street, which was lined on both sides with what remained of shops from the 16th century. They were stone cubicles with arched entrances—each cubicle must have held a shop. The arches and walls had collapsed, but the street still appeared as majestic as it would have been in ancient times.

"Jauhari Bazaar!" Nisha exclaimed.

"Imagine 400 years ago this street must have been filled with activity. Both sides lined with jewellery stores and people milling all around.

And then they heard it. Silencing through the sounds of the night crickets; the distinct sound of a galloping horse. It seemed to be growing louder as the sound traveled from the far end of the road. They could taste the bile at the back of their throats. The galloping grew louder and Chinmay shone his torch toward the source of the sound.

There was nothing. And the gallop turned into the trotting of a single horse, as if the horse had been alerted of the two people standing on the street. Nisha held Chinmay's hand. Her nails digging hard into the inside of his hand. They stood frozen.

Nisha was breathing fast and hard. Her face was white as she turned to Chinmay and hoarsely whispered, "Can you smell it?"

The invisible horse was now right beside them—they could hear its shoes hitting the stony path.

Chinmay nodded, trying not to make any sudden movement. He could smell the distinct odor that's associated with horses. Sweat, manure, and animal.

It couldn't be their imagination. Chinmay's heart was pounding.

"When I say run, turn around and let's head toward the gate as fast as we can," Chinmay whispered. Nisha nodded.

"One . . ." They say that horses can smell your fear . . .

"Two . . ." A loud neigh rent through the night . . .

"Three . . ." They both turned and ran as fast as their legs could carry . . . the light from their torches dancing maniacally on the road—two spotlights—scared like them—trying to not get caught by the other.

They suddenly felt something rush past them. It was the invisible horse that whizzed by. Chinmay's blood froze. He could distinctly feel the warm breath of the horse in the cold night.

Nisha dropped her torch . . . "Forget it . . . let's go . . ." Chinmay screamed.

*Nisha bent to pick it up and that is when she noticed . . . they were surrounded by glowing red eyes . . . lots of them!

She aimed the torch and gasped. Chinmay frantically shone his torch in all directions.

"Fuck!"

The screeching started. The sound of six black-faced and very agitated monkeys. A solo monkey walked into the spot of light created by Chinmay's torch—like a celebrity walking into the spotlight ready to perform.

Nisha gasped—"It can't be!"

It was the same monkey that Chinmay had thrown a stone at and injured. The monkey was rubbing the side of his face with one of its front paw. There was a dried, clotted wound at the same place where the stone had connected.

Chinmay's expression was that of disbelief— "How can it be? They are animals! They can't be ganging up like humans to take revenge!"

The simian had brought its friends seeking revenge!

The monkey screeched and exposed a set of very sharp teeth. Immediately as if on signal, the rest of the monkeys whooped and created a

---

*   If you want to read along the following portion that's marked in bold with its own background music, then scan the QR code to access the music and get ready to immerse yourself in the story.

noise that drove an icy nail down their spines. Chinmay and Nisha now stood back to back, moving their torches around. And in the spotlight coming into the light and disappearing into the inky blackness, were faces that were angry, and wanted revenge.

The simians had blocked off their exit toward Hanuman Gate as if they knew the duo was headed there. The troop of monkeys was now closer to them, forming an impenetrable ring of hatred.

They flashed their sharp fangs, drool dripping off from their chins. Their eyes glowed red. They didn't look normal. They were not acting normal. There was something otherworldly about them . . . like they were being controlled by some supernatural force . . . that had transformed them into almost human.

"We can't reach the gate; what do we do?" Nisha's voice quivered.

"We head back to Jauhari Bazaar and then get into the fort, and find some place to protect ourselves. In the open we are easy targets," saying this Chinmay gripped his torch harder—getting ready to use it like a club.

The screeching was now louder . . . Nisha and Chinmay were now sweating even in the cold winter.

"Nisha, you start running toward the fort. I will hold them back!" Chinmay whispered.

"I can't leave you alone," Nisha pleaded.

"Nisha think straight! We don't have time for arguments!" Chinmay's voice was stern mixed with fear! "When I say run, you run! Wait for me at the entrance of the fort. I'll meet you there! RUN!"

With that scream, Nisha ran as fast as she could into the darkness. The monkeys realized that one of their preys was getting away. They leaped at Chinmay with blood-curdling screeches!

Chinmay swung the torch and connected with the head of one monkey, which fell to the side whimpering. Another monkey clasped onto Chinmay's forearm, digging its teeth deep into the flesh!

"Aaaaarrrrrgggghhh!" Chinmay screamed in pain. He could see two of the monkeys trying to run past him and give chase to Nisha. He kicked one of them—catching it under its belly, which lifted the monkey off the ground and flung him at a distance. The monkey screamed in pain.

"FUCK YOU! YOU PIECES OF SHIT!"

Chinmay swung at another monkey that leaped toward him. He missed. The monkey scratched him across the face. Chinmay felt his face grow warm with the blood that now oozed from the side of his face. He grabbed the monkey by its throat and squeezed. Hard. There was spittle from his lips and blood that now drenched his shirt.

The monkey that had bitten into his arm kept scratching at him—shredding his shirt and drawing fresh blood! Chinmay could feel his adrenaline pumping—he felt no pain. His body was now in survivor mode.

Nisha stopped running when she thought she had covered a reasonable distance between the fight and herself. She turned to look over her shoulder, and all she could make out in the distance was the pin-sized torchlight dancing as Chinmay fought the rabid simians. In her head, the voice was that of sadness and regret.

"I shouldn't have insisted on coming here! I was stupid not to believe in all that we heard!"

She drank some water from her backpack and then checked out her surroundings. She shone her torch—it was wilderness and ruins. This building seemed different. It had layers to it. There was a flight of steps leading up to a clearing and then to the house. She checked her mobile phone for service, but there was no network, as Raghu had correctly warned them. She then checked the photograph of the map on her phone.

The house on her left was called 'Purohitji ki Haveli' or the House of the Priest. This is where the royal priest resided. It was about 500 meters or so from the watchtowers of the Royal Palace.

Chinmay squeezed harder, channeling all his anger into his grip. Another monkey, sensing that his brother was now slowly slipping into the void they called 'the dark world', leaped, grabbed, and scratched the arm trying to loosen the death grip.

Chinmay screamed and cursed. The monkeys fought back. As Chinmay squeezed harder and harder, he watched the monkey's eyes roll back in their sockets, its wide open mouth trying to grasp air, and the thrashing slowly subsided. Chinmay now let go of his grip. The monkey fell onto the stony path—dead and cold . . . and immediately the fight was sucked out of the other simians.

They all crowded around the dead monkey—screeching, whooping, crying.

Chinmay stood all bloodied, scratched, and angry. He screamed with all his force. He had won the battle between beast and man. The troop carried off their dead brother and vanished into the darkness.

Chinmay collapsed onto the ground. The adrenaline was now slowly fading away from his bloodstream and with that emerged pain. Sharp, shooting, excruciating pain.

Chinmay stood up and now headed toward the palace. He was glad that Nisha was unharmed. He was glad that he stood his ground to save her. But he could feel the energy fading from his body. He checked his watch—it was broken. Both his forearms were bleeding profusely. He took out his water bottle and tried to rinse off the blood.

He hissed in pain as the water cut through his wounds. He took off his jacket, and then his shirt. He tore pieces from his shirt and bound the cloth on both his forearms to minimize the bleeding. He knew he had to be strong so that they could survive the night and see the dawn of a new day.

Nisha decided to walk to the Royal Palace and wait at its entrance. Her body was shivering. She was scared. What she had envisioned as a fun walk in the park, had turned turtle, as she now realized that there may be some truth to the stories behind Bhangarh.

She quickly erased the thought from her head. She had to stay calm and positive. She walked up the sloping walkway toward the entrance of the palace.

"Nisha!" she heard Chinmay's voice coming from the darkness.

She screamed, "Chinu! I am here!" as she scanned all around her to spot him.

"Nisha, where are you?" Now the voice seemed to walk further away from her and now echoed from within the palace complex.

Had she missed seeing Chinmay crossing her while she had her back to the road, looking at Purohitji ki Haveli?

"I am here Chinu," she said as she now began to follow the voice into the palace.

Chinmay was struggling to walk. The weight of the backpack was now killing him. He decided to ditch the bag after taking out the bottle of water. He would pick it up on the way back, he thought. The pain in his arms was excruciating. He knew that a monkey bite could lead to rabies, but he had more serious things to do. He had to reach Nisha and get her to safety. He started walking faster. His entire body screamed in pain. And then he started running.

Nisha now stood at the base of a huge structure. She called out for Chinmay. She heard his voice replying and she saw a light pass inside the palace. She ran after it. She couldn't understand how Chinu could not hear her voice.

Chinmay stopped to take a breath. He could make out the silhouette of a structure in the moonlight. He shone his torch on the plaque outside the structure, and it read Purohitji ki Haveli. In the distance he could make out the dark shape of the royal palace perched high on the hillside. He resumed his trek.

Nisha was inside the palace now walking along the dark corridors, calling out Chinmay's name. Her voice echoed and bounced off the empty hallways and corridors. She put a hand to cover her nose, as the sharp smell of bat urine slapped her senses. She saw a light at the end of a corridor. She breathed a sigh of relief. Nisha called out his name as she started walking toward the light. As she walked closer, she could make out Chinmay sitting on the ground, hunched over. She was now worried. Had he been injured . . .

"Chinu, what happened? Are you hurt?"

Chinmay was now at the wide-open space in front of the palace. He swung the light across the area, calling out Nisha's name! She was nowhere to be seen.

"Nisha, where are you? Nisha?" he screamed.

Nisha was just a few feet from the man who was crouched. And then she noticed, that the light was not coming from a torch, but a candle. And the man was not wearing the same clothes as Chinmay. The man was wearing an orange shawl, like a priest.

"Chinu?" her voice quivered.

A low growling sound emanated from the man. And that is when she heard another voice calling out for her from somewhere in the distance . . .

"Nisha, where are you? Nisha?"

That was Chinmay's voice . . . then who was this man?

Her knees seemed to buckle from underneath her. She wanted to scream, but her voice was stuck in her throat. The groaning of this man grew louder. She watched transfixed, as the man now slowly started getting up from his crouching position. She tried to move and walk back . . . her feet were rooted to the ground . . . She was screaming as loud as she could—but only a hoarse whisper came out of her mouth . . .

The figure stood up with his back to her, and then slowly turned around.

Chinmay started panicking. Did Nisha lose her way amongst the ruins on her way here? Was she injured and lying somewhere? A thousand thoughts raced through his head. His heart was pumping and once again the pain subsided as adrenaline pushed into his veins. He screamed—"Nishaaaa!" His voice echoed through the empty village. In the distance he could hear the chattering of the monkeys float back to him.

Suddenly Chinmay felt a presence behind him. He swung around and gasped. In front of him was Chris.

"Chris! Oh my God! What are you doing here?"

Chris had a worried look on his face.

"I tried to help you last night! But you didn't listen! Why did you have to come?" Chinmay felt as if Chris' voice seemed to come from far away; like a hollow sound inside a dark cave.

"We thought . . ." Chinmay couldn't finish his sentence . . .

"Thoughts and thinking are for the real and rational world," there was pain in Chris' voice. Regret. Sadness.

"Chris, you have to help me find Nisha," Chinmay pleaded.

"It is too late! He has her! Just like he had me!" Saying this Chris turned around and began walking away.

"Chris! Chris! Don't go!" Saying this he shone the torchlight on Chris' back. His throat became parched. His knees buckled.

The back of Chris' head was lit up. It was hollow! There was a huge hole in his skull, with bits and pieces of brain hanging out. His blonde hair was matted with dried, coagulated blood, which made it stick to his scalp. Chris turned to look at Chinmay. Chinmay's scream was caught and silenced within his own throat. Only a hiss emerged from his mouth. Chris' face was no longer human. It was skeletal. Where his bright blue eyes were, there were black holes. His mouth was half, eaten away exposing his skeletal dentures. But the sadness was still visible on his face. Chris turned around, and then the night swallowed him up—embracing him into her dark folds to hide him.

Nisha was breathing heavily. The figure now was facing her. Nisha screamed her silent scream. The man's face was a mangled mess of rotting flesh. On his forehead was the fading mark of a priest's tika. One eye dangled from its socket— barely hanging on with the help of a few veins. Nisha could smell the fetid stench of a rotting corpse.

The man opened his mouth to reveal a black cavernous mouth—and when he closed it, blood dripped out from the side of his mouth. Nisha fell backwards and started crawling with her hands. The orange shawl fell off the shoulders of the man—revealing the body of a decomposed, melted corpse. The skin was eaten away in parts, while some of it melted and dropped to the ground when it moved.

The man lunged at her and caught her by her throat, and lifted her off the ground. It's growl now menacing, louder and hungrier. Nisha felt herself being lifted and her feet now dangling in the air, as she fought for her breath. The face was now close to hers. She could feel and smell its cold putrid breath on her face. She whimpered in fright. A dark, long tongue flicked out from the black, cavernous mouth and licked her face, like a reptile smelling its prey. Nisha could feel the life slowly going out of her.

A beam of light suddenly hit the man-creature's face. It growled in anger and looked at the source of the light.

Chinmay could not believe what he was seeing. Nisha was suspended in mid-air as if someone had lifted her off the ground. He could hear the growls of a creature but he could not see it. Chinmay rushed to help Nisha . . . and that is when the creature allowed itself to be seen by Chinmay. He brought his run to a sudden stop, his feet sliding out from under him. He now saw this hideous monster like man holding up Nisha. And its head now turned to look at him. Chinmay screamed— "let her go!" The man-creature dropped Nisha and lunged at Chinmay. Chinmay got up and started running—leading it toward him and far away from Nisha.

Chinmay rushed out to the open space in front of the palace and fell onto the ground. He turned to see the man-creature towering above him. It now lowered itself on its haunches and its face was now inches from Chinmay's face. Chinmay was palpitating. His entire life was flashing through his head.

He hated boarding school. He was always bullied.

He was now looking into the empty socket of the creature.

"Chinu, we are going to Disneyland in the summer holidays," his dad said.

The creature growled.

"I am so sorry, I am not going to be around for very long," his mom said from the hospital bed.

The drool-like blood dripped out from its mouth and fell on his face. He was finding it hard to breathe.

Valentine's Day.

Securing the top spot in the State board exams.

Looking into Nisha's eyes.

Watching the sunrise lighting up the Kanchenjunga.

Nisha giggling.

Cold seawater brushing his toes.

Nisha saying "I love you."

The man-creature now suddenly screamed and thrust his hand inside Chinmay's chest.

Chinmay had never felt such immense pain. He couldn't scream as blood started choking him from within.

Nisha saying—"Yes, I'll marry you!"

Their lips meeting.

Nisha throwing her head back with a scream as he hugged her naked body, sitting atop him.

He was now finding it tough to breathe. His body started to convulse. The creature pulled out Chinmay's heart with a blood-curdling scream . . .

As the world started growing dark around him he heard a deep, raspy voice say—"Bhangarh *mera hai*!" (Bhangarh is mine!)

Chinmay's body convulsed and then lay still. His chest was a wide, cavernous hole. Blood poured out of his body and seeped into the mud.

Raghu had arrived on time to pick up his guests. He had waited and then grown impatient. As soon as the guard arrived, he entered the village, searching everywhere for Nisha and Chinmay along with the guard. They found pools of dried blood outside Modon ka Haveli.

"This doesn't look good!" the guard said, as they quickened their pace, shouting "Nisha madam, Chinmay sir."

A little further ahead at the end of Jauhuri Bazaar, they found Chinmay's backpack. The road led to the palace. They started running. It was the guard who first spotted Chinmay's body.

Raghu on seeing the body with its chest ripped open, started to retch immediately. He sat on the ground. He couldn't move. He had never seen such a hideous sight in his life.

The guard ran into the palace and there he found Nisha sitting with her back against the wall, mumbling and whimpering. When the guard came toward her, she screamed in fright, trying to get away from him. It would take Raghu and the guard to calm her.

The site was closed for a few months till the investigations revealed that one of the monkeys had attacked and killed Chinmay. But what they couldn't explain was why was the body of the monkey and Chinmay found so many miles apart? And why would the monkey rip out the heart?

Nisha's parents came and took her back to Delhi. She told her parents about what happened in Bhangarh. But no one believed her. They thought the trauma of losing Chinmay had unleashed her imagination to cook up a story. She was admitted to various hospitals and mental-care institutions. She never recovered. Nisha now lives with her parents and is afraid of the dark. She keeps mumbling some gibberish about a priest who comes and throttles her in the dead of night!

AGRASEN KI BAOLI

A grasen ki Baoli, also known as Ugrasen ki Baodi, is a protected monument by the Archaeological Survey of India (ASI) under the Ancient Monuments and Archaeological Sites and Remains Act. It is a 60-meter long and 15-meter wide historical step well on Hailey Road, near Connaught Place, Jantar Mantar in New Delhi. Although there are no known historical records to prove who built Agrasen ki Baoli, it is believed that it was originally built by the legendary king Agrasen during the time of the Mahabharata and that the present architecture hints at it being rebuilt in the 14th century during the Tughlaq period of Delhi Sultanate. The Baoli is open daily from 9.00 a.m. to 5.30 p.m.

This Baoli, with 108 steps, is among a few of its kind in Delhi. The visible parts of this historical stepwell consist of three levels. Each level is lined with arched niches on both sides.

As you go deeper down the Baoli you will feel that the sound in there totally evaporates and what remains is only the silence and the echo of one's own footsteps. In the presence of deep silence, many visitors have experienced the presence of some unknown factor making people believe that Agrasen ki Baoli is the residence of the devils.

According to the sources, before the hay days of this place were over, the Baoli was filled with black water, which called out people's name mysteriously and asked them to sacrifice their lives in that black water. In fact, water was believed to enchant people to jump into it. Even today, these stories and incidents haunt this place.

Agrasen ki Baoli is said to be one of the top haunted destinations in India. Some people have said that they have heard strange noises and witnessed apparitions. However, no one knows the truth.

THE
MYSTERIOUS
SUICIDES

S hamita Mukherjee lay on her bed, wide awake, staring at the ceiling. Her forehead was covered in beads of sweat, despite New Delhi reeling under a cold wave. Nobody believed her. Not even her son—Karthik. Shamita of course, didn't expect her daughter-in-law Gayathri to believe her. Shamita knew that Gayathri had always hated her. And more so, since Shamita had moved into her son's house; into their three-bedroom apartment in the very prime location of Vakil Lane, Hamdard Nagar, after the demise of her husband Shamiran.

She had overheard Karthik telling Gayathri, "Where else will *ma* go? I can't let her live alone in Rohini. And she needs emotional support now!"

"But what about Rithik's studies? He is going to get disturbed, and where will ma sleep?" Gayathri was adamant not to allow Shamita to set up a tent on her turf.

"I'll clear out the third bedroom. It was always meant to be a guest bedroom, anyway. She is my mother, and I cannot let her live on her own. Let's get used to that idea," saying this Karthik had stormed off.

Shamita did not want to create a wedge between the two and she tried moving back to her flat in Rohini, but Karthik did not allow it. And with every attempt, Gayathri's animosity had increased.

And when the demons began whispering in her room, Gayathri had labeled Shamita as a senile lunatic who was undergoing emotional trauma, to overstay her welcome.

The demons began to visit two weeks ago.

Shamita remembered going to bed as usual, by 10.00 p.m., after having done a bit of reading. She had just discovered Murakami, and she had stood on the shore with Kafka. She switched off the bedside lamp. Sleep was not an easy commodity for her, and she had to take a sleeping pill to fall asleep. She had watched the light of the drawing room switch off, from under her closed door, as Karthik and Gayathri called it a night. The sedative pill had started dissolving into her bloodstream, slowing down her brain activity, lulling her senses, and cutting her off from the real-world. It was then, that she distinctly heard a whisper. It was a hushed female voice calling out her name.

"Shamita."

Her eyes slowly opened. She thought that it was her daughter-in-law coming in to her room to say something. But then why would Gayathri call her, by her name? She looked at her door. It was shut.

She could hear her own breathing in the silence. And then . . .

"Shamita!"

She heard the whisper again. It was crystal clear. It came to her from the corner of the room. She quickly switched on her bedside lamp. The sound of the switch sliced through the deafening silence. She looked all around the room.

How could walls speak? She brushed it away. Maybe it was the sleeping pill taking effect.

There was the sound of gurgling water that slowly began to envelop her from around her room. It was soft, inviting. As if her room had suddenly been transported under some water body. And then she heard her name again. This time the voice seemed to have traveled closer to her, and it was coming from the ceiling, just above her bed. She shook her head, trying to get the grogginess out.

Her heart skipped a beat. The warm, comforting, hypnotic, inviting gurgling sound of the water continued. And the voice whispered out to her—"come to me!" This time she wasn't mistaken.

She sat up in bed.

She ran out of her room and banged on her son's bedroom door. Rudely awakened, Karthik and Gayathri came to Shamita's room to check.

"Ma, you are just imagining things! There is nobody in the room, and there are no voices!" Karthik reassured her.

"This is really unfair ma! He has been working the whole day, and now you are pulling some tricks to get his attention!" Gayathri wasn't going to let go of a ripe opportunity to hit back.

"I heard it, *beta*! I promise, I heard a voice, and the sound of water!" Shamita pleaded. How could she convince them that what she was telling the truth?

"Ma, please *tumi shuye poro*! (go to sleep)" Karthik said. He was about to hug his mother when he felt a tug on his arm. Gayathri, it seemed, had had enough of this domestic drama, and she pulled him away.

Shamita stood alone in her room. She shivered for a few seconds—maybe it was her body trying to cope with the shock she had just had. She slowly looked around her room. Everything was normal. She slowly began to mutter the Gayatri mantra as she got into her bed.

****

Thud!

Thud! Thud! Thud!

Gayathri sat up in bed and checked her bedside clock. It was 6.30a.m.

"Has the upstairs neighbor started construction-work, or what?"

Thud! Thud!

The noise permeated through the walls of the house.

"*Suno! Utho!* Please go and tell the upstairs neighbor not to start work so early!" Saying this Gayathri tried to wake up Karthik.

Thud! Thud! Thud! Thud! Thud!

Karthik sat up; groggy-eyed. His eyes instantly widened in horror.

"It's not the Sharma's. The sound is coming from ma's room!" saying this he ran out of bed, closely followed by Gayathri.

They swung open the door of Ma's room. Karthik's blood ran cold. His mother was standing holding a metal vase in her hand. Her hair was unkempt. Her eyes—blood-shot with a look that was nothing short of pure insanity! The walls of the room had fresh dents in them, with paint peeling off and the cement and brickwork exposed.

"Ma, what is wrong with you? What happened?" Karthik rushed to his mother.

"You didn't believe me Karthik! But she came! She kept calling my name! She was calling me from behind the walls," Shamita's voice had an edge to it. She held on to Karthik's arm hard till her nails were digging into his skin!

"Ma, please sit down! It's just your imagination!" Karthik tried to reassure her.

"Ma, look what you have done to the walls! Added to the issue of the dampness in the walls, you have now gone and broken parts of it! This is . . ." Before Gayathri could finish her sentence, Karthik cut in, "Gayathri, please! Not now! Just ask Dr. Banerjee to come."

Gayathri stormed off. She couldn't believe the state of the broken walls! And she was fed up with Karthik always siding with his mother.

"You know I never lie to you, Karthik! I heard water move through the walls. And the voice . . . I can't be mistaken! I couldn't sleep through the night. I tried to chase her. I tried to catch her. But she kept getting away, and laughing!"

Shamita was exhausted. Her pleading eyes begged her son to believe. Karthik made her lie down. He slowly stroked her head.

"Please . . . please . . . believe me!" She said as tears streamed down her face.

Karthik spoke to her in a soft voice, "Ma, how can I believe you? And look what you have done to the walls. I am not going to hear the end of it from Gayathri."

Shamita broke down. "I am sorry *shona* for causing you so much trouble," she said, resting her hand on her son's cheek.

Karthik teared up seeing the state of his mother. Just then, a voice boomed from behind them, *"Aabar ki holo?"* (Now what happened?)

A portly man, with a bushy moustache walked in, carrying a leather attaché. It was Dr. Aviroop Banerjee. He lived on the sixth floor. It was always handy to have a doctor as a neighbor, and so he ended up treating patients within the building complex.

He checked Shamita's blood pressure.

"Mashima! This is unacceptable! It is too high! And what is this that Gayathri was telling me? You haven't slept the whole night! Do aaaaa! Take the tongue out! No wonder you are hearing things!" He checked her eyes with his torch.

"Everything except for pressure seems normal. She needs rest," Banerjee summarized his examination of the patient to Karthik. "Mashima, the sleeping tablets don't work for you, or what?" He asked Shamita.

Shamita was too tired to respond.

Banerjee just did "Hmmm!" And then prepared an injection. "With this, you will sleep for a bit! You'll wake up rested! *Bhawyer kono chinta nei*!" (No need to panic) Banerjee

46

assured Karthik, and pushed the needle into the frail arm of Shamita, who just emitted a 'ssss' as she felt the prick.

"Should we put her in an institution?" Gayathri whispered to her husband, once the doctor had left, "This is the work of someone who is mentally disturbed!"

"What happened to *Thamma*?" Rithik asked innocently, as he got ready to head off to school.

"Nothing beta! She is just a little unwell! You have a good day at school! Come, your school bus will be here in a minute!" Saying this Karthik took Rithik downstairs.

Gayathri slowly pushed the door to Shamita's room open. Shamita was fast asleep. There were chunks of loose cement, and peeled-off paint on the floor. Gayathri closed the door. In her mind, she thought, "We will get rid of her only when she dies!"

It was late at night when Shamita stirred in her sleep. Her pillow was drenched. She sat up and turned on her bedside lamp. And as she was wondering how her pillow had become soaking wet—a drop of water hit her forehead. She looked up to stare at the ceiling. The sound of gurgling water traveled from the ceiling to the floor. Shamita put on her glasses; a little groggy-eyed she looked to the floor.

She was astounded to see a pool of water. The water seemed to be coming from outside her room, and from under her bedroom door. *'From where did the pool of water come?'* she wondered. There was a deathly silence. And through that silence, a whisper sliced through taking her name.

"Shamitaaaa . . ." the whisper trailed off.

"Ke? Ke Okhanay?" (Who's there?)

The whisper called out her name again. It seemed to be coming from the door that led into the sitting room.

47

Shamita got out of bed and started walking toward the door. And something inexplicable happened. The pool of water seemed to come to life as it started retreating from her room and traveling outside. It seemed to be beckoning her, leading her.

Shamita called out for her son. Her voice emerged as a hoarse whisper that broke through the eerie silence. But there was no response. It was as if she was trapped in a vacuum from which no sound could escape.

She now followed the trail of water, which kept retreating on the floor, leading the way for her. Shamita distinctly heard a gurgle or was it a giggle? The voice beckoned her again.

Shamita followed the trail of water, as it retreated, under the door of the bathroom in the hall, with a loud gurgle. She stood there, unsure of whether she should venture further or not. She looked toward her son's bedroom down the hall. But she knew that waking them up now would only feed Gayathri's irritation.

The voice called out her name again. This time it came from inside the bathroom. Shamita slowly pushed open the door of the bathroom and gasped. The entire bathroom was enveloped in an eerie blue glow. The walls were alive with undulating patterns of reflection of water shimmering. The now familiar warm, comforting gurgle accompanied this strange spectacle. She felt compelled to see it. She had to see it. It was as if her feet were getting pulled inside. As soon as she stepped in, the door shut on its own. Shamita panicked; she tried to open the door—but it was jammed. Her heart was beating fast. She could feel her thumping heart try to push itself out from her aged, frail ribcage.

*And then a drop of water fell on her face. She wiped it. And another drop just hit her on the cheek. It was dripping from above.

She looked up to the ceiling from where the water was dripping. She stumbled back in fear at what she saw.

A woman was stuck to the ceiling . . . the water was dripping off the long strands of her undone wet hair. The woman had an ashen face. The woman's feet and hands were glued to the ceiling. The woman now slightly leaned forward to take a closer look at Shamita. This sudden movement took Shamita by surprise, and she tried to scream but only a gurgle came out of her throat. The same gurgle, which had haunted her.

The woman on the ceiling laughed. Shamita tried to undo the door once again. The door was still stuck! She felt an icy sensation on her shoulder. Shamita turned around to come face-to-face with the woman with the ashen face. The woman was now inches away from her face. There was a distinct smell of fungus and mildew that emerged from this woman . . . or was she a creature . . .

Shamita's brain froze. Shamita's body began to go into spasms of fright—and the ashen woman laughed, and as she did, more water

---

* If you want to read along the following portion that's marked in bold with its own background music, then scan the QR Code to access the music and get ready to immerse yourself in the story.

emerged from her mouth. The water dribbled down her chin and joined the pool of water already on the floor.

The woman now spoke to Shamita—"Come to me."

The sinewy hands of the woman emerged from under her saree. They had moss all over them. Shamita tried to scream as her arm was now in the icy, wet grip of this woman. She tried to resist, but it seemed futile. Shamita found herself being led by this woman toward the tap.

"Go on . . . don't be scared!" The woman said as she suddenly melted into a puddle of water.

Shamita tried to fight the urge. But she couldn't. She felt herself going to the tap and turning it on. The water started filling up in the bucket. And when the bucket was filled, Shamita mechanically turned off the tap. It was as if an external force was guiding her hands and actions. Her mind tried to resist. She was wondering why she was doing all of this. Her thoughts tried to take control of her body but failed. She heard the woman's warm, inviting voice again—"Come to me."

Shamita felt her knees go under, and before she could resist, she found herself slowly bending her knees and kneeling beside the overflowing bucket. It looked like she was praying to an invisible deity. Though she tried her best to resist, she found herself lowering her head into the bucket. She could feel the strangely warm water caress her face, and then consume her head. Her mind was racing—urging her to snap out of this reverie—to resist whatever was controlling her actions. Her open eyes were now staring at the stained bottom of the bucket. The water was warm and clear. She wanted to pull her head out of the water. But the force held her there. And then suddenly the clear water turned black. Shamita could no longer see, and she couldn't breathe. She struggled as water started filling up her lungs. She desperately wanted air. And then Shamita just gave in to the power that held her there. She stopped fighting it. She allowed the warm water to fill her lungs and replace every little bit of air that was there. The last thing she heard before life ebbed out of her was the ashen woman's voice saying, "Welcome home!"

****

The police inspector couldn't believe what he saw. It was surreal and creepy. When they removed Shamita's body from the bucket—her eyes were staring at nothing—and her mouth was wide open, her attempts to suck in the last gasps of air.

"It looks like suicide. It could be that she was depressed," Inspector Tiwari said, "having lost her husband recently."

Karthik looked at Gayathri for a beat. His mind was raging inside. Could his mother have gotten depressed because of Gayathri's taunts?

A chasm formed between the couple. And Rithik was told that his grandmother had gone back to her home when he had returned from school the next day.

"If you are going to hold me responsible for your mother's suicide—then I think it is unfair," Gayathri wanted to get it off her chest. It had been two weeks since the incident, and Karthik had stopped speaking to her completely. "She was already losing it—hearing voices, imagining things! Were you blind that you could not see, how her mental condition was deteriorating?"

Karthik just left her and walked away to the living room.

****

It had been two weeks since Tiwari had come face-to-face with the 'old woman drowned in the bucket' case. He just could not get the image out of his head. He was about to instruct the helper to serve him his lunch, when Chandlal Gupta, the head constable came rushing in.

"What happened? *Bhoot dekhe ho ka*?" Tiwari teased him, adding a Bhojpuri flavor to his tease.

"Sir, we just got a call about another suicide from Hamdard Nagar," he paused, whether for effect, or whether he couldn't believe the incredulousness of the situation; he continued, "It is a twenty-year-old boy. He was found drowned, with his head in the bucket!"

Tiwari and Chandlal hurried off to the crime scene. Tiwari's mind was racing. 'How the fuck could this be true? Maybe the kid fell down and hit the bucket?'

They rushed up the stairs to the house, and there, as they entered, they encountered a group of grievers, one of who pointed to the direction of the bathroom. Tiwari stood shell-shocked at what he saw. The boy was in the same position as the old lady.

"How could this be possible?" Tiwari first mumbled aloud, and then instructed Chandlal, "Check for any signs of break-in or forced entry. We need the statements of all the people in the house. And send the body for post-mortem."

The house was checked—there was no sign of forced entry. All the alibis were rock-solid. Tiwari just could not make head or tail about what was happening.

And it did not stop there . . .

11 deaths followed in the next two weeks . . .

When the posse of journalists surrounded Tiwari and asked him for answers, Tiwari's logical answer was, "This looks to be the work of a serial killer or they belonged to a cult. We are probing into it."

"Sir, when will you give us answers? Or will you wait for more people to die?" a male journalist hollered.

"How can a five-year-old girl be part of a cult?"

"The victims don't know each other at all!"

"Sir, is there some Baba they follow?"

"When there is no forced entry, how can it be the work of a serial killer?"

"Sir, stop bullshitting us with your answers! It is all a distraction!"

And that is when Tiwari lost the plot.

"*Teri maa ki . . .*" (You, motherfucker . . .) He lunged at the reporter, "*Behnchod! Tujhe jawab chahiye?*" (Sisterfucker! You want answers?)

Chandlal and other journalists pulled Tiwari off the hapless reporter. But the damage was done. Tiwari made it to the evening news on television, his video became a meme with *Tujhe Jawab Chahiye* emblazoned on the visual. And of course the news made it to the cabin of his superior, the next morning.

"What the hell was that Tiwari?" ACP Hemant Singh gritted through his teeth.

"Sorry, sir. That journalist . . ." Before Tiwari could finish, Singh interjected, "You have three days to find me this serial killer or get me some definite answers. Or else you will be managing traffic at the ITO crossing!"

****

Chandlal was hesitant, but he knew he had to say it, "Sir, *yeh koi aatma ya bhoot-pret ka kaam toh nahi hai?*" (Sir, could it be the doings of a ghost or an evil spirit?)

Tiwari looked up at Chandlal, and held his steely gaze. He then clenched his jaw and screamed, "GET OUT!"

Tiwari had been taught that every criminal leaves behind a clue. Unfortunately, for these 13 deaths—the criminal that he was dealing with had been very careful. The facts stared at him. There had been no forced entry in all the 13 cases. Which meant that the victims knew this person. There had been nothing robbed or stolen from the houses. Could it be a mass suicide? Nothing in their homes connected them—or to that one 'elusive' person who had gained entry to their homes. But more importantly, how could 13 unconnected people be connected with this one person? Who was this person?

Tiwari put his head in his hands and groaned. He could feel a migraine coming along, to further fuck his day up!

****

The maid, Sutapa was busy watching the afternoon repeats of a popular crime show on television. Sutapa was not her real name. Her parents had named her Bilkis, when she was born in Charghat, in the Rajshahi district of Bangladesh. Like many other Bangladeshi immigrants, she too had crossed over to West Bengal illegally in the hope of a better life. What she had quickly learnt was that her accent and her name, both gave her away. She cooked up a story of being a Hindu girl, and her accent being the result of being born in the border of Murshidabad. Two years later, she was approached by an 'agency' which promised her a good job in Delhi. And that is how she found herself working at the Mukherjees.

Karthik and Gayathri were at work, as every weekday demanded them to be. Rithik was busy playing in his room, sitting on the floor with his Lego set, trying to build a new house. When suddenly something cold touched his feet. He pulled his feet back to find that there was a puddle of water, where his feet had been just moments ago. In his little head, he wondered where this water had come from. And as he kept watching the puddle of water, it trembled and created tiny concentric ripples within it. Rithik crawled toward the puddle of water to get a closer look. It looked like any other puddle—like the ones that were created on the floor, when he had accidentally dropped the jug from his hands, a few months ago. He was about to go back to his under-construction house, when he heard a giggle.

It was the soft, melodious giggle of a little girl. Rithik looked around to see if there was any visitor who might have entered the room while he had been busy. There was no one. He could hear the distinct sound coming from the television in the living room. His mind rationalized that maybe the laugh had come from the serial that Sutapa *didi* was watching.

She never allowed him to watch cartoons in the afternoon and forced him to play in his room, or worse, fall asleep.

The giggle returned; and this time a small girl's voice whispered, "Come, play with me!" Rithik stood up. Was there somebody trying to play hide and seek with him? He rushed to peer behind the curtains, under the bed—but there was nobody. The puddle of water began to slowly move toward the door . . .

"Come, play with me . . ." the girl's sweet voice beckoned Rithik. He kept watching the water move. It fascinated him as well as puzzled him. He followed the puddle as it moved stealthily, invitingly across the floor. Rithik kept following it. He did not even realize that he had now entered the living room, and he walked by Sutapa, whose attention was seized by the serial on television.

Sutapa did not even notice Rithik walking past her—just ten feet away. The puddle stopped outside the door of the common bathroom. And then with a sudden jerk, it disappeared under the door, as if a vacuum cleaner had suddenly been turned on, sucking in everything in its path. Rithik pushed the bathroom door open.

He saw a little girl, the same age as him, sitting on the floor, and smiling at him. She was dressed in a green frock, and Rithik found it strange, that her hair was all wet, and plastered to her forehead, and the sides of her face.

"Come, play with me," she gestured for Rithik to come closer. Rithik stepped inside, as if in a trance, and came closer to the girl. The girl now pointed toward the bucket. And as if the girl was mentally passing on instructions to him, Rithik turned the tap on and watched the bucket fill up with luminescent blue water. It looked beautiful.

"It is beautiful, isn't it?" The girl said as if reading Rithik's mind, "Now put your head inside, and you will see a magical world!"

****

Sutapa switched off the TV as the serial ended and got up to check on Rithik.

Not finding him in his room, Sutapa called out to him. But there was no answer.

"Stop hiding now! I don't want to play hide and seek with you!" She announced. But there was no stirring within the house. She checked all the rooms again.

****

Rithik did not know why he was doing it, but he found comfort in the soft voice of the girl. He liked listening to her. Kneeling down in front of the bucket, which was now overflowing, he slowly held the sides of the bucket with both his hands.

"Don't be afraid . . . Go on . . . You will love it!" the voice assured him.

Before he could dunk his head in the water, he turned around to look at the little girl. His eyes widened in horror. In the same place where the little girl had been seated, was now a woman with scaly skin, wet hair, and white eyes that had no pupils. She laughed with a rasp that made Rithik petrified. He screamed . . . but he could feel as if some power was pulling his head toward the bucket. And before he could resist any longer, Rithik found that he was staring at the bottom of the bucket. His head was surrounded by the blue glow. And then the water turned inky black! Rithik gasped for air—and his lungs started filling in with water.

The last thing he heard was a scream . . .

****

When he next opened his eyes, Rithik saw that he was lying in his bed, and the face of Dr. Banerjee looming in front of him, slowly came into focus.

"Good boy," Dr. Banerjee smiled, and then walked out with Gayathri to the living room, "How did this happen?"

Through tears, Gayathri narrated the events.

Sutapa had found the bathroom door locked from inside, and she had screamed for Rithik. When there had been no response, she had managed to shove the door open using all her might. And she had frozen for a second, seeing Rithik with his head in the bucket! She had screamed and had pulled him out. Sutapa got the water out of his lungs and placed a call to Gayathri.

"This doesn't seem right!" Banerjee shook his head and a frown formed on his forehead, fast-forming wrinkles emerged quickly—like a mountain range was being formed with the sudden push of tectonic plates.

"Your mother-in-law may have been depressed . . . but the series of suicides that have been plaguing the area in a similar way—and now this . . ." Banerjee, usually a rational man looked up and said, "This could be a paranormal occurrence."

Gayathri burst out, "What do you mean? My son just tried to drown himself and you are calling it paranormal? Maybe he has seen the news reports on television and wanted to try it, like any normal child!"

Dr. Banerjee nodded his head and said, "If there was a rational explanation to all of this—how come the police are unable to find answers; and unconnected people choosing to die in the same way? Please ask Karthik to call me once he gets home."

Saying this Dr. Banerjee left. Gayathri's head felt like a million flies were buzzing inside it. She sat next to Rithik and held his hand. A tear rolled down her cheek.

Rithik looked at his mother and said, "Don't worry Mama, I am fine! She will not be able to take me away from you!"

A chill ran down Gayathri's spine. She asked him, "What did you say? Who will not be able to take you away from me?"

"The woman with the long hair. The woman who wanted me to go inside the water," Rithik's voice was now a whisper, as if he was afraid that the 'lady' would be eavesdropping.

Gayathri's voice rose a little, "What nonsense are you talking about? It was all your imagination!"

"No Mama! I saw her. In the bathroom, and she said . . ." At this point Rithik altered his voice to a hoarse whisper, and repeated, "Come play with me!"

Gayathri shrieked and shrank back in fear. Her hand hit the photo frame that was on the bedside table. It crashed to the floor, and the glass broke. Gayathri was hyperventilating! Hearing the crash, Sutapa rushed into the room, "*Didi, Ki hoyechay?*"

Gayathri looked at Sutapa with a blank expression, and her voice quivered, "Nothing. Nothing happened." Gathering her senses, she instructed Sutapa to clean up the mess. She walked into the sitting room and dialed Karthik's number.

Karthik was a little surprised to see his wife calling him up at an odd hour. She was probably going to apologize, he thought. It's not going to be enough, he told himself. He disconnected the call, and returned to his work. His phone rang again. He was now a tad irritated. He picked up the phone and hissed, "Why are you calling me . . ." And before he could finish his sentence, he was silenced by one word—"Rithik."

"What happened to him?" Karthik yelled as he started looking for his car keys.

"Just come home. Please come home," Gayathri begged him. Her voice was a mix of fear and panic.

****

Karthik drove like a man possessed. He was just ten minutes away from his house when he was forced to screech to a halt. There was a traffic jam, filled with incessant horns blaring. He thumped the steering wheel in frustration and cursed. He waited for 30 seconds, hoping that the traffic snarl would ease. But no luck!

He stormed out of his car to see what was holding up the traffic, and his feet landed in a puddle of water.

"Fuck!" He cursed, seeing his only pair of Hush Puppies now drenched in water. And then he realized that it was not a puddle that he had stepped into, but a mini stream, which had popped up. The water was flowing down the street and was already reaching the top of the heel of his shoes!

"*Bhaisaab, ho kya raha hai?*" (Brother, what's going on?) he yelled at the taxi driver, who had steeped out of his vehicle, in front of him.

"*Sadak repair ho raha tha! Saalon ne water pipe burst karwa di hai!*" (They were repairing the road, but the swines have damaged a water pipe) The taxi driver replied, hocking a mouthful of phlegm into the running stream. Karthik saw the blob of phlegm floating toward him in the water, and quickly stepped out of its way.

He got back into his car, dialed Gayathri and told her the situation.

It would take him another hour to reach his home.

****

Once he reached home, Karthik rushed in and hugged his son. Rithik could not clearly fathom why his parents were suddenly so agitated and were giving him so much attention.

Karthik made Rithik sit on his lap, hugging him, ensuring that his son felt a sense of security.

"Can you tell us, what you saw?" Karthik asked, softly.

Rithik described what he had seen, a few hours earlier . . . the water, the voice, the lady, the beckoning, the force, the lady . . .

Dr. Banerjee, Gayathri, and Karthik hung on to each of the words that came out of Rithik.

Goosebumps prickled his skin. He felt his stomach tighten up into a painful knot. His eyes welled up with tears. But he could not understand whether it was out of sheer concern for his son, or fear on his part.

Gayathri had requested Sutapa to stay back for the night. But Sutapa had scampered off saying, "*Iss ghar mein bhoot hai!*" Gayathri had tried to reason with her, but Sutapa was out of the door and frantically pushing the call button of the elevator used by the servants and non-residents of the building. And before Gayathri could say anything more, Sutapa had hopped into the elevator, and the doors had slid and closed on her, and she was gone.

Now they were all huddled, listening to Rithik tell them, what seemed to be a story straight out of a fantasy horror film.

"Rithik," Karthik cajoled him, "You are sure that you did not . . ."

"NO! NO! NO! I DID NOT IMAGINE IT! WHY WON'T YOU BELIEVE ME?" Rithik burst out, taking all of them by surprise. He burst into tears. Karthik pulled him into his chest. Rithik buried his face there and cried.

****

There was silence in the room, which was cut by the sound of ice cubes clinking against the insides of the glass. Dr. Banerjee twirled the old-fashioned glass in his hand. The amber whiskey glowed in the dimly lit room, as the light of the table lamp seeped into the drink. He was thoughtful. Karthik had his head in his hands.

"Now that you know what is at stake here, I will get in touch with Mishraji. I am sure he will be able to help," Dr. Banerjee, took a swig of the last dregs from his glass and got up to leave.

"Shouldn't we be informing the police?" Karthik asked.

"And tell them what? About a ghost who asks people to drown themselves in water? And the inspector will believe every word you say and award you?" the doctor was losing his patience. Banerjee just could not understand why Karthik and Gayathri were not getting it!

"We are dealing with something that the police or logic will be able to comprehend or combat." Dr. Banerjee finished the remainder of his drink in one gulp.

"Take the day off tomorrow. I will get Mishraji to come," saying this Dr. Banerjee left.

****

The rotary phone had rung ten times before someone picked it up at the other end.

"Hello, Mishraji *hain*?" (Is Mishra-ji there?) Dr. Banerjee asked.

A feeble voice answered, "*Dete hain. Kaun bol rahe hai*?" (I'll give the phone to him. Whom should I say has called?)

"*Unko boliye*, Dr. Aviroop Banerjee *ne phone kiya hai . . .achcha nahi, nahi . . . unko boliye Pavan-putra Hanumanji ka phone hai*!" (Tell him this is Dr. Aviroop Banerjee. Hang on, tell him it's the Son of the Wind God, Hanuman)

"*Eh? Kya?*" the man at the other end was puzzled, no doubt, "*Mazaak hai kya?*" (You think this is a joke?)

"*Arre unhe bata dijiye—wo samajh jayengay!*" (Just tell him—he will understand) Dr. Banerjee chuckled.

There was a pause for three minutes, as Banerjee held the mobile to his ear. He heard the faint noise of someone coughing and then the receiver was picked up.

"A true devotee, need not do anything more than just take my name, with pure devotion and chaste mind, and I'll be his support in the darkest of times," Mishra ji repeated the famous lines of Lord Ram.

And they both burst out laughing.

"You are still the scoundrel!" Mishra said, his laughter a mix of mirth and phlegm.

Banerjee and Mishra had both studied in the same school in Kolkata and for two years in the senior school play—Mishra had enacted the role of Lord Ram, while Banerjee had played the role of Hanuman.

After pleasantries were exchanged, a sense of somberness gathered between the lines.

"You calling me after 10 years, and at 11 in the night—I am sure it is not to practice your lines . . .What is it Avi?" Mishra asked.

Mishraji, or Akhilesh Vidyuth Mishra, was a paranormal expert. He had studied the Vedas, had lived in the mountains for years, and then realized his calling. He had returned to Delhi and had set up his office in Darya Ganj. The shop was just a hole in the wall. He knew that he would have more dial-in clients rather than walk-in ones. Over the past 25 years, his fame as a ghost-buster had grown. The people, who believed in him, swore by him. While the other lobby of disbelievers, predictably called him out as a fake money-guzzling pretender-shaman.

His appearance was far from that of a traditional shaman. He dressed in jeans and checkered shirts, throwing a denim jacket on when the temperature dipped. He had snow-white hair—unkempt, unbrushed, and unruly.

Banerjee told him about the death of Shamita, the other deaths in the locality, and what happened with Rithik. Akhilesh listened intently and then, in a stolid tone, said, "I will be there by 11 in the morning."

And just when Banerjee was about to hang up, Akhilesh piped up like an epilogue, "Lunch is on you. I haven't had Bengali style mustard fish in a long while!"

Akhilesh was born in Calcutta. And Ronju his other best friend (apart from Aviroop) introduced him to the non-vegetarian culinary masterpieces during the annual Durga Pujo—Fish fry, Kosha Maangsho, and other delights. When Akhilesh's parents found out that their son had done '*dharam-bhrasht*' they were shell-shocked, and threatened him with dire consequences if he ate non vegetarian food again. But Akhilesh did not mind risking meeting the devil in his father as eating a dim-er devil gave him far greater pleasure. And so he had to find opportunities to quench his hunger for Bengali food on the sly.

Banerjee laughed, "I'll feed you good Bengali food tomorrow! You first reach on time . . . Don't be late like the time when you had to attack Lanka and you went off to take a leak . . . the war was delayed!"

They both burst out laughing.

****

There was a crowd gathered around 602.

Tiwari stood and watched as the ambulance boys lifted Dr. Banerjee's lifeless body onto a stretcher. This is ridiculous, he thought to himself.

Chandlal cut through the crowd and approached Tiwari, "Sir, he lived alone. His wife had passed away 10 years ago. Very helpful fellow."

"That's not answering my questions, Chandlal! Where is that friend of his who came to meet him today after 10 years?"

"He is in that flat, where the old lady killed herself. 403," Chandlal continued, "I spoke to him, and he said that the doctor had called him up last night."

"That is strange," Tiwari bit his chapped and darkened lower lip as he chewed on his words, "Doctor calls his friend after 10 years out of the blue, the doctor is found dead in the morning, and then the friend is sitting in the house where the first suicide took place!" Tiwari ran across the facts aloud.

He just couldn't put his finger on the pulse. It kept vanishing. "Get forensics to lift fingerprints. I need to chat with this friend."

Saying this Tiwari walked out of 602.

****

Akhilesh had nothing to hide. And so told Tiwari about the school days, and how he had met Banerjee. And about the strange phone call last night.

"But why did he call you? And how come you are sitting here with people you don't even know?" Tiwari was at his wit's end. The facts were staring right at his face and yet he was trying to poke holes in them—in the hope that something would emerge.

"Banerjee wanted me to look into the death of Shamita— and as soon as he told me about the deaths in the locality, I knew that they had to be connected,"

Akhilesh spoke slowly. His eyes were a crimson red from having cried on seeing Banerjee kneeling beside the bucket, with his head submerged in the water. The security guard had called from the intercom, to let Banerjee know that he had a guest. When there had been no response, the security guard, along with a few neighbors, had broken down the door, only to discover that it was too late.

"Connected?" Tiwari seemed taken aback. After all, he had seen all the jigsaw puzzles—but he had been unable to fit them together, "But how?"

"Water."

"What kind of an answer is that? Of course, they are connected by water—they all drowned!" Tiwari replied.

"Do you believe in ghosts and spirits, inspector?" Akhilesh looked Tiwari straight in the eye and shot the question.

"*Bakwaas hai!*" (It's nonsense), Tiwari flared up, "This is the work of some serial killer! And ghosts and spirits do not exist! Please don't feed me that hogwash!"

"Do you believe in God, inspector?" Akhilesh said, calmly.

"Of course I do! *Yeh koi poochne wali baat hai?*" (What kind of a question is that?)

"But you have not seen God—how can you be so sure that God exists?"

"It's faith! It's belief! Humans have always believed in God from time immemorial!" Tiwari was now really losing his patience!

"From the early Mesopotamian civilization to the ancient Egyptians, Greeks, Indians, and Chinese. Even the Bible has mentions of ghosts. Do you see the oxygen in the air? NO! But we breathe it! Just because you do not understand it or see it—doesn't mean it does not exist!"

Akhilesh, who had just suffered the emotional trauma of losing his childhood friend, now realized that he was sitting opposite a fool, and trying to make him understand things that were completely out of the inspector's realm of understanding.

Tiwari was quite taken aback by the outburst.

"Have you ever heard of the word *Sheekol Buri* or *Jol Pishach*?" Akhilesh asked as he toyed with the gold ring on his index finger. It was that of the symbol Om, a diamond dotted the crescent.

"What are these?" Gayathri asked before Tiwari could respond.

Akhilesh turned to Karthik, "You must know about them. They are from your part of the country."

Karthik nodded, "Yes we have heard about these when we were young . . . when I visited my grandparents' house in Baruipur—there was a pond there. We weren't allowed to go near it after sunset. The villagers said that a Sheekol Buri lived inside the pond."

Gayathri and Tiwari who were both non-Bengalis couldn't figure out what the other two were conversing about.

Akhilesh now bent forward, as if he was about to share some secret knowledge, which of course he did. Akhilesh turned to Tiwari, "Now listen with an open mind. Sheekol Buri or Jol Pishach are spirits that dwell in water bodies. They are said to be the spirits of young women who had a tumultuous marriage or who committed suicide by drowning. Then, to seek revenge for their own deaths, these spirits lure people into the water, where they drown them, and claim their lives."

There was pin-drop silence in the room. Tiwari, felt an itch at the back of his throat, but dared not clear it.

"I believe that the deaths in this locality are being caused by a Jol Pishach. But why suddenly and where has it come from, are the two questions that I need an answer for," Akhilesh now leaned back against the sofa.

Tiwari could not believe what he had just heard. He laughed out. A hesitant one, at first. And when the ludicrousness hit him, he guffawed. Akhilesh kept watching him with a tiny smile on his face.

Tiwari controlled himself, "So what do you propose?"

"That you continue to do your investigation, and I will do mine. Your world and mine are different. Unfortunately, a crossover has happened. And I need to look into it," Saying this Akhilesh got up and looked at the silent Mukherjees who had been sitting and watching the war of the words play out in front of them, and said, "I will be here at 9 tonight!" And Akhilesh was gone.

Tiwari sat there for a while quite dumbfounded at the exchange that just took place. He cleared his throat and got up, said a courteous goodbye to the Mukherjees and he too exited.

****

Akhilesh looked at the large printout of a map on the wall. It was the map of Hamdard Nagar and the neighboring area. He had spent the last 6 hours culling data from the internet about the deaths and had meticulously stuck red pins for every death that had occurred in the area.

Akhilesh had to rely on the only eyewitness account that was available—Rithik's.

He went over the conversation that he had with him . . . the receding water . . . the voice . . . the lady with the long wet hair . . . the force . . . the water turning black . . . the water turning black . . . why did that sound familiar . . . *kala-paani* in the Andamans . . . no that wasn't it . . . the black water . . . what was it?

Akhilesh knew that it was a water spirit . . . but why this sudden manifestation from out of the blue . . . why now?

Akhilesh closed his eyes and replayed the conversation and the details he knew—and all he could visualize was water . . . water . . . His inner voice reminded him—the Jol Pishach needed a water body to inhabit . . . Akhilesh's eyes flew wide open . . . that's it! He peered into the map on the wall to find the closest waterbody near Hamdard Nagar. He quickly opened up Google Maps on his laptop. He typed in 'Hamdard Nagar, New Delhi.' The image immediately zoomed in. He cursed under his breath—the map had taken him to a different Hamdard Nagar. He typed in Vakil Lane. This time it took him to the correct locality. And what Akhilesh saw on the screen made him freeze. He felt a little short of breath suddenly. His mind told him that he should have realized it sooner. And his head told him what a fool he had been. He now kept zooming in till the computer screen was filled with the location and its description.

Agrasen ki Baoli—historic step well with stone arches.

Akhilesh took the cursor and then dragged the yellow man from the bottom right corner and dropped him on the location to get a street view of the place.

Immediately his screen filled up with a 360 degrees photo of the step well. He sat there staring at the arched step well.

And all the jigsaw pieces started assembling inside his head.

****

"Agrasen ki Baoli. That's the cause of these deaths," Akhilesh was seated across the Mukherjees.

"I don't understand—how could it be connected?" Karthik was floundering in the woods, so to speak.

"The stepwell was supposedly built in the times of the Mahabharata, as we have heard. Then it was reconstructed in the 14th century. When it used to be filled with water, in my younger days; the water used to be black—dark, evil, and mysterious. Frightening too. There has always been the myth of this Baoli being haunted—and how people have been lured into its waters, never to emerge again. It's all falling into place now. For years, the Baoli has kept drying up—only the deepest recesses of the Baoli have water—and that is probably where the Jol Pishach resides."

Akhilesh stopped to look at their expressions and whether they were taking all of this in. The Mukherjees were looking at him like two goldfish in a fishbowl—their mouths slightly agape, their eyes wide in wonderment.

"When Rithik mentioned the waters turning black—it immediately took me back to my childhood memory of the Baoli—and how we were not allowed to visit the Baoli after 5.00 p.m.—lest we get lured into the inky, black waters! Even now, no one will dare enter its premises after dark!" Akhilesh took a sip of the water from the glass in front of him. He waited ten seconds, to catch his breath, and then continued, "But the second question was bothering me—How did this spirit who was living all these centuries in the Baoli, suddenly find her way into the locality? And on the way here—I found the answer."

Gayathri softly asked, "What is it?" As if she was too afraid to find out what the answer was going to be.

"Come with me," saying this Akhilesh walked to the balcony and he pointed out to an area down the street, "That is your answer!"

Karthik and Gayathri could see some yellow lights, construction boards stating 'Men at Work' and some machines digging out the mud.

Akhilesh realized that he was dealing with slightly slow people.

"That construction work has been going on for the past two months—they have been trying to repair the road and inserting new water lines. I spoke with the engineer in charge. While they were digging, they accidentally dug into a chasm that was filled with water. What they didn't know is that this chasm is connected to the Baoli. The water from the Baoli has now access to all the homes in the area as it has entered the main water-pipe!"

"We should tell the inspector," Gayathri was alarmed, hearing Akhilesh spell out doomsday.

"And he will immediately welcome us and believe every word we say?" Akhilesh was acerbic in his response, knowing fully well that Tiwari would treat this as a joke.

The night was torn apart with the sound of an ambulance ripping through the locality. The trio rushed to the balcony to see an ambulance and a posse of police cars halt outside a neighboring housing complex. From their 4th-floor balcony they watched as inspector Tiwari got out of the police jeep and rushed into the building along with his deputy.

"Another one . . . she claimed another one tonight!" Akhilesh sighed, "I need to talk to the inspector. Maybe there's a way I can explain it to him." Saying this he walked out of the flat, and into the elevator.

****

"You want me to do what?" Tiwari looked at Akhilesh, incredulously.

"You have to get the municipality to change the water-piping of the locality."

"Are you out of your mind? Do you know how ridiculous it is going to sound, when I tell them that . . .?" Tiwari did not even bother finishing the sentence. He could not even get himself to say it!

"Alright then, you are going to keep having more bodies turning up," Akhilesh issued the warning and walked away.

Chandlal who had been privy to the conversation, piped in, "Sir, *maine aap ko kaha tha . . .*" (Sir, I had told you so . . .) Tiwari just gave him a look of disdain and got into his police jeep. Chandlal watched Tiwari drive off.

Chandlal looked around to see where Akhilesh was and spotted him getting into his car. "Sir! Sir!" he screamed to get Akhilesh's attention. Chandlal ran up to him.

"You have also come to make fun of me?" Akhilesh asked with a smirk that reeked of resignation.

"*Nahi* sir! I have come to tell you that I believe you!" Chandlal said as he tried to catch his breath. Akhilesh was taken aback. "That's new!" he said sarcastically.

"Sir, in our village too there used to be a pond, inside which resided a spirit. She used to devour the children who dared to bathe in that pond. Is there something we can do to stop this?" Chandlal looked genuinely concerned.

"I need a few things that I will need you to get for me . . . and I need access to the Baoli post midnight tomorrow. Bribe the security guard. And no one needs to know," Akhilesh handed over some money to Chandlal, and then scribbled a note for him, "Meet me at midnight tomorrow at the Baoli entrance."

Chandlal was about to walk off, when Akhilesh said, "Chandlalji, I hope you believe in God!" Chandlal was taken aback at this sudden question on his faith, at such an inopportune moment, but he replied, "*Haanji* sir, absolutely. I am a *bhakt* of Hanumanji."

"Good, because we will need all the Gods to be protecting us tomorrow!" Akhilesh patted Chandlal on his shoulder, and they parted ways.

****

Akhilesh was tense. He knew that he was dealing with an entity that could kill him. He had never faced such a demon before.

The table lamp cast elongated shadows on the wall as Akhilesh paced up and down in his study. He had a plan . . . but he wasn't sure whether it would work or not. It was all up in the air.

He went to a safe in the wall. He hesitated a moment before he opened it. He reached into the dark safe and pulled out a green glass bottle. There were two large blood-red sapphires encrusted on the sides of the bottle. The sapphires winked at Akhilesh as they caught the light.

The sapphires had a history to them. Akhilesh had traveled to Tanzania many years ago to study the indigenous tribes. He had lived with the oldest tribe of Tanzania—the Datooga tribe close to Mt. Hanang. The tribe is known for its blacksmith skills, beadwork, and making ornaments.

When the shaman had asked Akhilesh what he did for a living, Akhilesh had told him, with the help of a translator, that he fought demons and ghosts. The shaman had laughed out loud showing off his toothless gums. They were alike, the shaman had said. And when it was time for Akhilesh to leave after spending three months with the tribe, the shaman had gifted him the two red sapphires, as a farewell gift. The shaman had said that the two sapphires dug from the belly of the earth, would always guard him against evil. Akhilesh caressed the sapphires with his fingers—they strangely felt warm to the touch, even in this winter cold—as if they were burning from within—thus creating a fiery red glow.

The green bottle dated back to the 10th century or what is known as the Middle Ages. These bottles were known as 'witch bottles' and were used to trap spirits and demons. Akhilesh had found it in an old shop in Gloucestershire when he had gone to attend a Wiccan coven there. He knew that he would need it tomorrow. He peered inside and then shook the bottle. The old rusty nails inside the bottle rattled against the glass sides to emit a clanging noise.

Akhilesh knew he would have only one chance to capture the spirit . . . if not . . . he shook his head; he didn't even want to think about it.

****

Akhilesh checked his watch. It was 10 minutes past midnight. He was on edge. The temperature had dropped drastically. He pulled his overcoat tighter. He blew his own breath into his palms to keep them warm. Akhilesh looked like a smoke-spewing dragon in the eerie light cast by the streetlamp. Was Chandlal going to turn up, or had he chickened out? Maybe he had been sent by the inspector to patronize and humor him. Akhilesh looked around for the security guard. Thankfully he was not there. Maybe, Chandlal did bribe the guard, after all.

Akhilesh watched a light come from the end of the road. It glowed brighter as it came closer. It was a three-wheeler. Chandlal emerged, apologizing profusely. He pulled out six jerry cans from the auto. He looked triumphant, like a son showing off his marksheet to his parent, "I have got what you wanted."

The auto driver looked at the two men standing in front of the Baoli entrance. He was puzzled beyond belief, "What are you two doing here? Don't stay here! It is haunted!" Saying this he zoomed off.

Chandlal and Akhilesh carried the jerry cans inside the Baoli. There was an eerie silence all around. The darkness was absorbing every bit of sound. There was a light fog in the air. Chandlal shivered. He could not make out whether it was his body trying to adjust to the temperature or was it because he was scared.

They walked to the top of the stepwell. It was so dark that they could not see anything at all. The 108 steps leading down to the well seemed to vanish and melt into the darkness within a few steps.

From a satchel, Akhilesh took out a high-powered flashlight and turned it on. The beam of light bounced onto the distant wall of the step well, hitting just below one of the arches. Immediately there were loud screeching sounds, followed by loud fluttering.

"Bend down," Akhilesh screamed. Both Chandlal and he ducked in time, as hundreds of bats came screeching and screaming out of the dark shadows and flew past them. The sharp, acidic smell of the bats wafted into their noses.

"Now watch your step," saying this Akhilesh started walking down the steps into the depths of the well. He had gone a few steps, when he realized that Chandlal was not there with him. He swung around and aimed his flashlight at the top of the stairs. The beam of light caught Chandlal squarely in the face. There was utter panic on his face.

"What happened? Come on down!" Akhilesh said. His voice echoed across the cavernous and eerie well, and bounced off the walls. It sounded like the walls were all speaking at the same time.

"Do I need to come down with you? Can't I wait up here?" Chandlal was not taking any chances. The memories of the haunted pond from his childhood were playing on his mind.

"I cannot do this alone. We don't have much time!" Akhilesh was getting impatient.

Chandlal hesitated for a beat and then started walking down the steps toward him.

When they reached the bottom of the stairs, Akhilesh placed the bottle with the sapphires there. Chandlal watched, puzzled at the proceedings.

Akhilesh then started emptying out the liquid from the jerry cans. He first emptied one to make a large circle with the bottle at the center. He then instructed Chandlal to open the cans and start pouring the liquid and keep climbing back up the steps.

Like Hansel and Gretel's breadcrumbs, the two of them traced two straight lines with the liquid, from the bottom to the top.

They sat down at the top of the steps. They were out of breath. Suddenly they heard movement at the bottom of the well. They were alert. Akhilesh shone the torch toward the source of the sound—but there was nothing. They waited. Only the sound of the night crickets could be heard.

"Chandlal, remember my life is in our hands. When I tell you, you move . . . like we have discussed . . . you move as fast as lightning—we have only one chance!" Akhilesh was a little jumpy as the time neared for him to act.

"Don't be scared! And don't listen to the voice!" Chandlal already seemed to have fazed out! Akhilesh slapped him, which immediately brought back Chandlal to his senses, "Look at me! LOOK AT ME!" Akhilesh screamed . . .

"DO NOT LISTEN TO THE VOICE! DO WHATEVER, BUT DO NOT LET HER GET INSIDE YOUR HEAD!"

Chandlal nodded. And then he promptly got up and ran to the side and vomited. The fear was trying to exit from the inside.

Akhilesh suddenly had a sense of regret, taking on Chandlal as his partner for this. Chandlal came back, wiping his mouth with a handkerchief, "*Ho Jayega* sir! (It will be done, sir.) I will do it."

"If you get scared, just chant the Hanuman Chalisa . . . you believe in Him. He will protect you!" Akhilesh paused for a beat and took in a deep breath and then exhaled, "Let's do this!"

Saying this Akhilesh started walking down the steps and into the inky darkness. Each step echoed and multiplied. Chandlal could just see a white beam of light dancing in the dark as it descended—the sound slowly fading with every step.

Akhilesh reached the bottom of the 108 steps. Nothing happened. He turned around to look back up the steps. Chandlal was a tiny silhouette standing akimbo.

And just then, Akhilesh heard the soft, warm gurgle of water coming from the innards of the ancient stepwell. A sense of unease settled in the air. He turned around. There was a blue glow that was throbbing and growing brighter as it slowly emerged from within the dark cavernous space under the arches.

A soft laughter . . . like the voice of a little girl . . . echoed . . .

"Come home to me . . ." the voice said as Akhilesh stared at the arch, waiting to come face to face with the Jol Pishach.

The voice wafted up the steps enveloped in an ominous sibilance and reached Chandlal. Hearing the voice—Chandlal immediately began reciting the Hanuman Chalisa. He could feel beads of sweat run down the sides of his face, despite the biting winter cold.

Akhilesh watched as the blue glow flooded the floor of the well and from within the glow emerged a shape. With gurgles and sound of water the shape lifted its head. It was a woman. Where her eyes should have been were hollow black holes. She smiled at Akhilesh.

"Come to me . . ." she whispered with an animalistic growl.

The voice seemed so comforting that Akhilesh could feel himself slip into an abyss . . .

He struggled to be in the moment . . . the Pishach laughed . . .

Akhilesh started mumbling the incantation under his breath to protect himself. He started walking backward. He tried to focus on the task at hand. The Pishach lifted her sinewy hands with the long fingernails and beckoned to him. Her wet hair was plastered along the sides of her face and fell in long endless tresses on her hands and fell behind her like the trail of a wedding gown. Only this one was ghastly.

"Join me . . ." the Pishach invited him. Akhilesh continued to chant the incantation—it grew louder and louder, as he tried to prevent her voice entering his head.

The Pishach now looked up and spotted Chandlal . . .she hissed. The serpentine sound echoed and traveled up to Chandlal who could feel his throat tightening in fear.

He could hear her voice inside his head. It beckoned him. It invited him. He could feel his knees go weak—the world seemed to fade away into an inky blackness. Chandlal collapsed, lost and hypnotized by the warm, soothing voice.

Akhilesh screamed—"Chandlal, get up, GET UP!"

The Pishach cackled in glee. She tilted her head to one side and stared from her hollow eyes at Akhilesh. Akhilesh who had been walking backward felt the first step behind his heel. The Pishach sensed something was wrong and stopped.

Akhilesh screamed, "NOW! NOW!"

Chandlal could hear a voice coming from very far away, the Chalisa slowly dying on his lips . . .

Akhilesh screamed—"CHANDLAL! DO IT NOW!"

Chandlal could feel the scream jolt him as he woke out of his stupor and stood up. His head felt groggy. The Pishach growled in anger as she started walking toward Akhilesh.

Chandlal took out 2 small blowtorches from Akhilesh's satchel and fired them on! He bent down and lit the two lines of the liquid that they had poured earlier! The lines of petrol immediately fired up and raced down the steps. Chandlal smiled and collapsed to his knees. He had done his job.

Akhilesh started running up the steps, as the lines of fire raged past him on both sides. And before the Pishach could realize, she was trapped within a ring of raging fire. She screamed!

The Jol Pishach tried to step out of the ring but the flames locked her in. Akhilesh screamed his incantations aloud. The flames reflected on his face giving it a red glow.

Seeing there was no way she could escape, the Jol Pishach shape-shifted and entered the blue bottle. The red sapphires glowed like two eyes! Seeing this, Akhilesh leaped into the ring of fire and closed the lid of the bottle and screamed, "INTERIUS MANEAT IN AETERNUM!" (Stay inside forever!)

He picked up the bottle and realized his legs were on fire. He stumbled out, holding the bottle in his hands. Chandlal raced down the steps and tried to put out the fire with his shawl. They both lay down on their backs, drained of physical strength. They knew that it was finally over.

****

Chandlal reported for duty with bandaged palms. When Tiwari asked him what happened, Chandlal smiled and said, "I was helping with cooking at home. Picked up a hot *dekchi* by accident!"

"You are an idiot!" Tiwari barked at him. Chandlal just smiled.

****

Akhilesh wheeled himself out of the elevator. The Mukherjees were waiting for him with the door to their flat open.

"What happened?" Karthik asked.

"It's a long story!" Akhilesh smiled a tired smile.

Deep inside the safe of Akhilesh's house, the blue witch-bottle shook, rattling the nails inside.

****

ABBOTT MOUNT

A remote place in Uttarakhand is a favorite place for ghost hunters. The interest of TV news and documentary filmmakers have made Abbott Mount, at Lohaghat in Champawat district, famous.

It is known for the mansion and the derelict hospital.

It is believed that the Morris Hospital was established in late 1930s. The place has all the ingredients—a haunted hospital, a neglected church, and a graveyard—to create curiosity. Villagers tell the tourists about the supernatural forces operating during the night. The ghost stories used to keep people away from the mansion! But, off late, tourists have started invading the spookiest place. Earlier, they used to watch the hospital from a distance, but now visitors enter the premises to make videos and take photographs.

Local myth has it that the derelict hospital building is haunted. A Dr. Morris is said to have done bizarre experiments there and his patients or victims now haunt the place. It was said that the doctor could predict the exact day when a particular patient would die. In truth, he would shift them to Mukti Kothri—another cottage where he would conduct experiments on them, till they died.

THE HOSPITAL
OF DEATH

2005

Shirish, Sneha, Rafique, Naaz, and Raghav were all students at the same college in Lucknow. With the college being closed for the Christmas and New Year holidays, the gang decided to take a holiday together.

Shirish was the group leader—the good looking alpha-male. At 5'11 he towered above the rest of the group. Excellent goal-keeper and lawn-tennis champ, he was the prize catch of the college. He had decided to concentrate on his studies, ignore the advances of the many girls who sent him notes or SMS messages. He enjoyed the attention, but he didn't want to commit to a relationship. But that was a year ago. Last year his vow of studiousness met a juggernaut called Naaz.

Naaz had joined in the second year. She had arrived from Aligarh when her father had been transferred to Lucknow. She had wanted to stay back and complete her college in Aligarh—but her strict father would have none of that. He liked to keep things right under his nose and within sight.

Shirish remembers the day vividly like a favorite scene from an oft-watched movie. As Naaz stepped into the classroom, Shirish noticed that she was wearing a white *chikankaari salwar-kameez* and had the *dupatta* over her head. When she entered the class, she removed the dupatta from her head. The teacher had taken the note from her and had introduced her to the rest of the class.

"This is Naaz Sheikh. From today she will be joining the class," Mr. Rathod the Economics teacher had announced. Naaz's light grey eyes searched for an empty seat—and that's when her eyes landed on Shirish. For a beat they had held on to each others' gaze till she quickly looked away and sat down a few benches ahead of him.

It would take two months for Naaz to finally start talking to Shirish, and another two months for him to realize that his heart had betrayed him. He knew that she came from an orthodox Muslim family and he from a radicalized Hindu one—and that this love story was not possible. But he had held on to a glimmer of hope somewhere deep in his heart.

Sneha became Naaz's confidante and best friend. And that's how Naaz's parents had agreed to allow Naaz to go on this trip. The official story that was narrated to Mr. Sheikh was . . .

"Only girls are going for this trip. It is an excursion to Lohaghat to study the culture and the history for a project. Boys are not allowed on this trip."

Mr. Sheikh had given it a thought for three whole days, before he had succumbed to the emotional blackmail of his wife, "How long will you keep her caged? In Aligarh she had no friends, because of you! In this new college—at least let her have some friends!"

When Naaz broke the news to the gang, Shirish smiled and both of them had looked at each other from the corner of their eyes—*could this be the moment that they had been waiting for?*

Sneha was the bubbly extrovert of the group—she had a loud voice and a loose tongue. Boys were scared to take any *panga* with her. She would not hesitate to abuse them, often reminding them about their mothers and sisters with the choicest epithets! She never believed in love and relationships, which she referred to as *'bloody bakwaas.'* So when she saw Naaz getting attracted to Shirish—she had had a word with them separately to remind them to not waste their time.

Rafique was the muscleman of the gang. He worked out when he wasn't in class. He was stocky and dark-skinned. The sweat glistened on his skin like beads of black pearls when he worked out at the college gym. The biggest regret in his life was his height—or the lack of it! He wasn't a devout Muslim. He had stopped going to the mosque since his mother had passed away five years ago!

"I stopped. What is the use of praying when there is no justification in why it was my mother who was chosen to die in a freak car accident?" That was his logic, tinged with emotions.

She had gone to the ATM to withdraw money. When she was about to cross the road, a car driving on the wrong side of the road had slammed into her. She hadn't even seen it coming!

Shirish and Rafique were in fact childhood friends. They had gone to the same school and were now in the same college.

"Let political parties spread hate politics—*lekin asli* India *hum hai*—nothing can divide India!" They had embraced.

Raghav was the studious nerd. His nose was always buried in books. He was the backbone that everyone relied on when they needed notes, extra classes, or guidance. He was a 'man of science' looking for logical reasoning behind everything. Raghav was from a family of doctors and engineers and therefore had been looked upon as a black sheep when he had decided to pursue management. But his understanding father had stood up to his brothers and had allowed him to pursue his dream.

This was the gang that checked into Hotel Paradise in Lohaghat, after making the train journey from Lucknow to Kathgodam, followed by an almost 5- and-a-half hour drive up the mountains.

"It's nice and cold," Sneha exclaimed as she buttoned up her jacket.

"We are expecting snowfall in a day or two," the receptionist said with a smile, "Lohaghat looks beautiful in the snow!"

"I have never seen snow in my life!" Naaz said softly.

"Then you should hope the predictions are true!" Shirish said with a wink.

And so the gang roamed around Lohaghat in a hired car taking in the sights.

"Are you sure you all want to see it?" Rafique asked the gang, "We should be checking out the famous haunted Abbott Mount!"

"There is nothing called ghosts! It's just our imaginations

that make up things!" Raghav justified, "If you are in a dark room, alone, you will start to imagine things! It's human!"

"But you can't deny the fact that villagers have heard voices, screams coming from there, multiple times! How can everybody imagine the same thing year after year?" Sneha put her argument on the table.

Raghav cleared his throat before he launched into his speech, "You all have obviously not heard about Émile Durkheim," he paused to see their blank faces.

"Hmm, thought as much! So he was a French sociologist who came up with the term 'Collective effervescence' which describes the behavior of a community or society that comes together to simultaneously communicate the same thought and participate in the same action—it is a collective behavior that excites individuals and unifies them! It makes them seem relevant and together!"

"So you mean to say—they all imagine the same thing because it makes them feel part of the same experience?" Naaz asked.

"Something like that! There must have been legends and lores—and now the villagers keep it alive—maybe for tourism purposes!" Raghav explained.

"So what's the decision?" Shirish asked dramatically like he was Hamlet, "To visit Abbott Mount or not to visit Abbott Mount that is the question!"

They all decided that their trip to Lohaghat would be incomplete without a visit to one of the most haunted places in India—Abbott Mount and Mukti Kothri.

On the way to the Advait Ashram, the tourist car driver, Rajpal narrated the story of the Abbot Mount or The Abbey to the gang after much hesitation.

"Why waste your time going there?" Rajpal said while negotiating a curve on the road, "It's not a good place!"

The gang looked at each other as if they had found hidden treasure.

"But you can at least tell us the history of the place, no?" Rafique asked.

Rajpal remained silent for a beat. Perhaps mentally undecided whether he wanted to break open Pandora's Box, or not! He took a deep breath followed by a long sigh and began, "The place is known by many names—Abbott Mount, The Abbey, Mukti Kothri, and Morris Hospital. Well there was Mr. John Abbott who built this place around early 1900s. His main house, called The Abbey, and his farms were in Jhansi. The family resided in Jhansi except for the summer season when they would all come up to Mt. Abbott.

Locals also called this place The Abbey although it wasn't its name. John Abbott was heavily invested in Jhansi, including building dams to support the railroads and irrigation works. He also started the Hume Pipe Factory in 1925 which manufactured cement water pipes. Locals used to say that Abbott saab loved to spend time here gazing at the eternal snows of the Himalayas.

As rumors go, around late 1930s, is when we know, the place was converted into first an orphanage and then a hospital. In a place like Lohaghat where good medical facilities were not available the hospital became very popular with the locals. A few years later a new doctor arrived—Dr. Morris. Some say he was just a regular doctor, others believed that he was a neurosurgeon," Rajpal slowed the car down, rolled down his window and hucked a mouthful of red *gutkha* spit.

"Do you have to do that?" Naaz asked disgustedly!

"Madam, gutkha keeps us drivers awake! We drive sometimes 12 hours a day. Or else we will fall asleep at the wheel!" Rajpal justified his disgusting habit and action.

Naaz screwed up her nose and said, "Okay, continue the story!"

Rajpal continued, "There are many missing details about this place—no exact date when the mansion was converted into a hospital. Even the family members are not sure that it was converted into a hospital or not! People have forgotten about John Abbott—all we now remember is the evil Dr. Morris!"

"Why evil?" Sneha asked.

"You see, there were rumors that this doctor could foresee the future."

Raghav smirked, "It's getting better—the ghost story now unleashes Nostradamus!"

"Whose what?" Rafique asked with an expression of bewilderment.

Raghav thought he better tell Rafique about the French seer and astrologer who lived in the 15th century, but then decided against it. He lacked patience.

Rajpal continued, "He had a divine power. So by looking at his patients he could predict what was going to happen to them! And inevitably he always said that they would die! What kind of a stupid doctor he was!" Rajpal laughed at his own statement, and then continued, "So just before the patients were predicted to die, he would transfer them to a separate cottage, which is about a mile from Abbott Mount where the patients could live out their last days! This cottage became known as Mukti Kothri—the place where the souls would become free!"

The air in the car suddenly felt stifling.

"Could we open the windows—let's get some fresh air!" Naaz said, and as a warning to Rajpal, "And please don't spit your gutkha! It will come back to us!"

Rajpal smiled looking into the rearview mirror, exposing his red, stained teeth.

They rolled the windows, and immediately the crisp breeze hit them, carrying a faint smell of pine trees.

"Locals soon began to suspect that Dr. Morris was deliberately killing the patients to keep his predictions alive and believable. But then another story started emerging . . . It seems, Dr. Morris was interested in the occult—and he was eager to find out about what happens to humans after they die. What happens to the soul and the mind at the exact time of death? And, therefore, he used to perform occult surgeries on these patients. Killing them one by one, as predicted on the day of their death!" Rajpal looked at the rearview mirror to fathom the expressions on the faces of the tourists.

"And that's how Abbott Mount and Mukti Kothri became haunted by the souls of all these people who had been killed! You will see a church there as well. It was built by John Abbott in the memory of his wife. It is locked up and in ruins. And there is a graveyard there as well where Abbott was buried in 1945." Rajpal finished his story.

"So don't the locals go there?" Raghav asked.

"No. We avoid the place like the plague! Why take a chance with disgruntled spirits?" Rajpal said as he slowly drove into the driveway of the Ashram.

"This is bullshit! There is no thing as ghosts and spirits!" Raghav said.

Rajpal smiled, "For you city folks it is easy to dismiss it. But for us who have been living for generations in Lohaghat—it is true! We all believe in it!"

Raghav thought for a while whether he should repeat the 'collective effervescence' theory, but realized that it would not be well received by Rajpal, and so he let it go.

After much back-and-forth discussions, the gang decided to hike up to the village above Abbott Mount. The village offered spectacular views of the Himalayas. And en-route they would drop in at Abbott Mount just for a cursory look.

"Just a look. And we are not staying there for too long!" Naaz had made it clear.

They got food packed for the hike and off they went. The distance to the village was just over five kilometres. But for the city slickers, it seemed like an endless climb. The temperature was warmer than usual. It almost felt like they were back in Hazratganj.

They came upon an iron gate that had two white crosses on them. And beyond that lay a long path—which once would have been a glorious driveway. The gang looked at each other and there seemed to be an air of trepidation which Raghav broke as he stepped forward and pushed one of the gates open. It was rusted and difficult to push. The bottom portion had gotten stuck in the mud. Shirish stepped in and both of them pushed the gate open. The bottom of the gate created a perfect arc in the mud, as if it was a geometrical compass.

The path in front of them was strewn with dried leaves and overgrown with moss and weeds. The sounds of the crickets filled the air.

"Listen to the crickets chirping!" Sneha said.

Raghav cleared his throat and said, "Well this sound is produced when male crickets rub their leathery front wings together to attract female crickets as mates. It is called stridulation."

Everyone looked at Raghav.

"What?" Raghav asked, and then realized why they were looking at him, "Listen, I can't help it! These facts keep popping up in my head!"

"*Saala*, Encyclopedia!" Rafique said and thumped Raghav's back.

Their feet on the dried leaves created a rhythm that added to the sound of the crickets. Almost like the sounds of a percussion instrument being overlayed on a bed of strings. They didn't speak to each other—probably apprehensive about what to expect. From the main walkway, they took a left and there in the distance they caught their first glimpse of the Abbott mansion.

It was a single storeyed long structure, with red tin roof. It resembled more of a hospital than a mansion.

"Bwhahaha," suddenly Shirish let out a loud evil laugh to scare the others.

Naaz, Rafique, and Sneha jumped in fear and then pounced on Shirish, "That was so mean!"

They walked toward the mansion. The breeze whistled through the trees in an eerie whisper. They now stood under the front portico of the building with its long corridor. All the doors and windows had been jammed and barricaded with planks of wood.

"The walls have been cemented recently. So somebody obviously is looking after the property," Raghav said. They tried to peer inside the building through a broken window. All they could see were a few broken wooden beds and hospital side tables.

Rafique lit up a cigarette, "It's lovely smoking in the hills! Such fresh air!"

"Yes, which you are proceeding to pollute with your smoking!" Naaz rebuked him.

Shirish's hands brushed against Naaz's, and they exchanged looks and smiled. They were at the back of the pack. Shirish leaned over and quickly gave a peck on Naaz's cheek.

Naaz's eyes went wide in mock horror! She quickly paced up her walking to join the others in the front, lest Shirish get further excited and proceed to do something more drastic and demonstrative.

They walked around the building and went toward the back. The building did not look colonial at all. In fact with the new cement work and a hideous black, giant Sintex water tank on its roof, the building could have passed as something constructed in the last 20 years or so.

The old brown brickwork of the place was interrupted by patches of white cement which looked like a repair job. Suddenly Naaz gasped and pointed. Her eyes were wide in horror! They all looked toward where Naaz was pointing and Sneha shrieked.

There was a writing on the wall with what looked like dried blood. Shirish took a step forward toward the wall to get a closer view. Naaz grabbed his hand, "Don't go!"

"Chill! I am just going to read what's written!"

Shirish and Raghav stepped closer to the wall to read the semi-faded writing. The note was written in Hindi and it read, *'Dhyan rahe aap nazron se'* (Beware of the watchful gaze).

"Looks like some idiot tourist who wrote it to spook people!" Raghav said dismissively.

"But it could have also been written by one of the villagers, warning tourists about the spirits!" Sneha argued with a trembling voice.

"You girls are being paranoid!" Rafique said as he took a last drag from his cigarette and threw the butt on the ground.

"Come on! Let's check out the church and the graveyard!" Shirish led the gang away from the hospital toward the abandoned church.

"Do we really need to visit the graveyard?" Naaz asked, "I mean, we wanted to see the hospital. We have seen it. We should head back now!"

Shirish laughed. "We have come so far. We might as well see it. And Naaz, this is not a zombie film where ghosts will suddenly emerge from the graves!"

A well-timed 'boo' from Rafique made the two girls leap in fright and scream!

They walked toward the church. The birds that had been chirping suddenly fell silent.

The abandoned church was a beautiful stone structure with a hooded entrance with green pillars. They got closer to it. Naaz and Sneha understandably were at the back of the group.

Raghav brushed the dirt from the marble plaque at the entrance wall and read aloud, "Dedicated to the memory of Mrs. Linda Abbott. Erected by her husband. 1942."

Shirish peeped through one of the broken windows of the church. The pews were all dusty and scattered. A lectern stood amidst the pews. There were broken pieces of wood, a few hymn books lying on the ground. It was as if the inhabitants left in a hurry.

They suddenly heard a thud. They froze. A shrill cry of a bird rents through the air. The bird startled by the sudden noise took flight. And again a thud! They all looked at each other. They slowly walked toward the sound. And again, a thud!

Naaz whispered, "Forget it! Let's go back!" But the boys were not interested in listening to her. They tip-toed toward the sound. And then it stopped, as if the source of the sound had been alerted about the presence of the strangers.

The group stopped in their tracks. Raghav pushed his way to the front, turned around to face his friends, "Why are you all spooked? Chill! I will go and investigate if your courage seems to have deserted you!" Saying this Raghav climbed up the stone steps and walked back toward the hospital.

Thirty seconds or maybe less, Raghav's scream exploded and tore through the silence!

They all ran and then almost skidded to a halt. Raghav was on the ground, and standing above him was a burly man, wearing a sweater that had seen many good days, but was now held together by patches of multi-colored swabs of cloth. And in his hand he held an axe!

They stood there shell-shocked. It took them a few seconds to realize that this person was not a ghost. The man held out his hand toward Raghav who took it and the man helped him to stand up.

"I turned the corner and bumped into him!" Raghav explained.

The man asked in a gruff baritone, "What are you children doing here? Don't you know you are trespassing?"

"We were just seeing the place . . . we had heard about it . . ." Naaz said.

"Heard what? That this place is haunted?" The man asked as he swung the axe over his shoulder.

"Yes . . . Yes . . ." Shirish said.

The man looked up at the gathering clouds in the sky and said, "There are no ghosts. Just old women's superstitious tales! You better hurry back to town. There is a storm coming!"

The gang looked at the man and nodded.

"But the driver had told us . . . ." Rafique began, but was cut short unceremoniously when the man took two steps toward them and said in a slow menacing tone, "There are no ghosts! GO!"

They rushed off walking toward the driveway.

"That man gave me the creeps!" Naaz said as she hugged herself, suddenly feeling cold.

"I thought he was a ghost when I turned the corner and bumped into him!" Raghav said sheepishly.

They all looked at him! "But I thought you didn't believe in ghosts!" Rafique said!

"*Bhai*, it was so sudden. By the way, I still don't believe in ghosts! As you can see the man turned out to be real!" Raghav, it seemed, was getting his confidence back.

The driveway was deathly quiet as if the mute button had been pressed. There was a flash of lightning. Immediately Raghav started counting, "One thousand one, one thousand two . . ."

"What are you counting for?" Sneha asked.

"It's Physics! "Raghav was multi-tasking. He was conversing with Sneha and in his mind he continued to count.

The roll of thunder growled menacingly.

"One thousand six!" Raghav stopped and did a mental math. They were all looking at him. "The storm is less than two kilometers away! We need to hurry!"

"How do you know that?" Rafique asked!

"It's simple! You need to count the number of seconds between the flash of lightning and the sound of thunder. Light travels faster than sound—and that is why we see it first, and then we hear the thunder. What you count you need to divide by 5 and you'll get the distance in miles or kilometers to the lightning. I counted to 6 seconds. Which means 6 divided by 5 gives me 1.2 miles, which is about 1.9 km."

"Fuck! What were we doing in school?" Shirish said jokingly!

They walked out of the rusted gate. They all looked back at the driveway.

"Goodbye Morris Hospital!" Shirish said. And just then the first one hit Rafique!

It was a hail the size of a walnut. Thankfully, it had landed on his shoulder and missed his head.

"*Maa ki Aankh*!" Rafique screamed. And they looked all around them to see the hail coming down in sheets of white.

"We won't make it!" Naaz said. They all looked at her and stopped in their tracks.

"Lohaghat is almost 5 kilometers away. We will get drenched and with visibility being poor—we may even fall off the side of the mountain!"

They turned to look at the Abbott Mount over their shoulders.

"We should wait in the shelter of the hospital till it stops," Raghav continued, "And listen it's not haunted—we have realized that."

"Maybe we can ask the old man where the nearest village is—we could go there and get some food," Shirish wanted to get out from the pelting that they were receiving, and get into a shelter.

They all ran back to the shelter of the Hospital.

"Sit here. I will go and search for the guy," saying this Raghav disappeared.

"Let's gather some of the old wood that we can find and see whether we can start a bonfire. Look the woodcutter has left behind some of the logs," Rafique pointed out.

A few logs had been piled up at the corner of the veranda.

The temperature was rapidly dropping. There was mist coming out of their mouths when they spoke.

"See I am smoking without a cigarette!" Sneha joked as she let out a breath of mist from her mouth.

It was getting dark. They gathered a few twigs, dried leaves and bits of broken wood that they could find and Rafique lit a small bonfire on the veranda.

"That man is not there," Raghav returned.

"Where could he have gone—he was there just 10 minutes ago!" Naaz was puzzled.

Suddenly the noise of metal scraping against the floor made them freeze. A cold shiver ran up their spines.

"Did you hear that?" Sneha whispered, a little shaken.

There was silence. And again the prolonged sound of something metallic being dragged across the floor broke through the stillness.

"It sounds like . . ." Rafique began the sentence, and let it hang as if he didn't want to complete it and thereby confirm what he thought it was.

But Sneha completed it, "One of the hospital beds being dragged!"

There was a flutter of panic amongst them. Naaz was visibly shaking.

"Don't panic! It probably is something metallic grating against a surface," Shirish tried to quell the panic.

"We shouldn't stay here. I have a bad feeling about this," Sneha's voice quivered as she spoke.

Rafique got up, "I am sure that old man is trying to pull a prank on us to scare us away. I am going to go and take a look."

"Don't go!" Naaz pleaded.

"I am going to be fine," Saying this he pulled out a burning log of wood from the bonfire, "I will burn the motherfucker who is trying to scare us!"

Before anyone could react, Rafique walked away. They all watched the amber glow of the fire as it slowly grew smaller as Rafique walked away, and then disappeared around the corner.

An owl hooted in the forest. The cacophony of the hail hitting the tin roof of the derelict hospital was loud. They had to almost scream and talk to overcome the din.

It was pitch black. Nothing was visible around them. The driveway was enveloped in darkness. The fire reflected on their faces, and it cast ghostly dancing shadows on the wall of the hospital.

Naaz thought she heard a noise and looked over her shoulder. She assumed that it was Rafique coming back. But the end of the corridor was dark. And that is when her eyes fell on the wall—and she shrieked. On the wall were five shadows seated around the fire, even though there were just four of them.

"What happened?" Shirish said and came toward her.

Naaz was shaking and hyper-ventilating, "The . . . the . . . wall . . . shadows . . ."

They all looked at the wall to see their own shadows embedded on the old and dilapidated wall.

"It's just our own shadows," Sneha said, "Why did you get spooked?"

"There were FIVE shadows. I swear I saw five shadows. There was someone sitting with us."

"It was just your imagination," Shirish argued.

Naaz yelled, "It wasn't my imagination! I know what I saw! If you don't believe me—that's fine!"

"Why isn't Rafique back yet?" Raghav looked worried.

"I think we should just get out of here. Let's go and look for Rafique and then leave!" Sneha was scared to her bones.

Shirish thought for a beat.

"Alright. Let's do it," saying this Shirish picked up a burning log and so did Naaz. They now walked gingerly, following the path that Rafique had taken.

"Rafique! Rafique!" They all screamed his name out in turns.

Sneha held onto Raghav's arms tightly.

With no Rafique in sight—they were worried.

"Where has he disappeared? I hope he hasn't fallen off the cliff at the back!" Raghav seemed stressed, as his mind started assuming the worst possible situation.

"Okay this is what we do. Naaz and I will go down this way. You two go the other way, and we will both meet at the back. That way we would have covered the entire perimeter of the building," Shirish laid out the plan.

"No! We should not separate. Please!" Sneha was petrified.

"It's okay Sneha. I am there. We will be fine," Raghav assured her.

With much trepidation in their hearts the group now broke into two pairs. The veranda was once again enveloped in darkness as they went their separate ways, their fire torches became tiny dots and were swallowed by the dark of the night.

"Rafique? Stop messing about! Come out. This is no time to play pranks!" Shirish was on the edge.

"There!" Naaz said pointing her fingers. Down the corridor—there was an open room from which a warm glow emanated.

Shirish laughed, "He thought he could hide! Idiot! His fire gave him away! Come on," saying this he held Naaz's hand and they walked toward the room.

As they neared the room, their feet slowed down with the realization there were voices coming from the room. A woman was speaking with another man.

Naaz clamped onto Shirish's hands like it was a lifeline. Her throat felt parched.

'How was this possible? There was nobody on the property?' Shirish's mind was racing.

And just when they were about ten meters away, a woman stepped out of the room.

Naaz and Shirish could feel the bile in their mouth. In front of them stood a nurse with a bloodied apron holding a medical tray in her hand.

Their mind screamed, *'RUN!'* But their feet were frozen to the ground.

And then slowly, the nurse turned toward them—her head cocked to one side. Naaz screamed, but only a hoarse, guttural sound emerged from her throat.

The nurse stood there watching them for what seemed like an eternity. And then her mouth opened to let out a blood-curdling scream and all of a sudden she charged toward them. Naaz and Shirish ran in the opposite direction as they screamed. Their feet felt heavy, and they found it difficult to run.

And suddenly they both fell backward as they collided with something heavy in the darkness. They fell back on the ground—the fire torch was dislodged from their hand. It lay on the ground; its glow diminishing with every second as it started dying.

****

*The hailstorm had stopped. The ground was covered in the white clumps of hail, which shone like diamonds as the light from the fire-torch illuminated them in the darkness. Raghav and Sneha walked toward the rear of the hospital calling out Rafique's name only to be met with a deafening silence. The only sound was the crunch of the hail under their feet as they walked. It was as if they were in a vacuum and all the sound had been sucked out.**

"How could he have just disappeared into thin air?" Raghav was now befuddled.

"Raghav, this place is really haunted. We should just get out of here and come back in the morning," Sneha kept looking over her shoulders. Her instinct told her that they were being followed.

---

*   If you want to read along the following portion that's marked in bold with its own background music, then scan the QR Code to access the music and get ready to immerse yourself in the story.

"Sneha. It's all urban myth and legend—probably done to boost tourism. There are no ghosts!" The pragmatic and realist Raghav refused to be sold the story of Abbott Mount being haunted.

Suddenly Sneha grabbed Raghav's arm and whispered in a shaky voice, "Raghav there is someone behind us . . ."

Raghav swished around and held up the fire torch—but there was nobody. Sneha had broken into a cold sweat. And then she distinctly heard someone breathing next to her—and she felt someone brush past her. She shrieked. Raghav turned to her, "Sneha you are just imagining things!"

"I swear . . . I swear there was somebody!" Sneha was crying in sheer fear.

Raghav took out his cell phone and then cursed, "No bloody network!"

A dim light glowed in the distance. It was the light coming from a naked bulb.

Raghav pointed toward the light, "That's the abandoned church. Do you think Rafique headed that way?"

"We should go back Raghav. Let's not go there alone. We should take Shirish and Naaz as well," Sneha pleaded.

Just then they heard Naaz screaming in the distance. They looked at each other in fright. But before they could react . . . an invisible force from nowhere yanked Sneha. She screamed.

She thrashed and tried to set herself free, but to no avail. Raghav stood frozen to the ground. A helpless statue. Sneha was dragged about 20 meters and then she disappeared into the night where the graveyard was located. Her screams fell silent.

Raghav wanted to scream, but nothing came out of his mouth. And then he vomited. He broke down like a baby. He swung his fire torch around to see if there was anybody. His sobs sounded like grunts of a wounded animal. He ran and retraced his steps to catch up with Shirish and Naaz.

Shirish and Naaz looked around. There was deathly silence. And the nurse was nowhere to be seen.

"Quick! Pick up the torch before it goes off!" Naaz could barely speak. Her throat felt parched, and she could hear her heart thumping in her chest.

Shirish picked up the torch and lifted it up to throw its glow as far as he could. There was nobody, except for them.

He turned around and held out his hand for Naaz and that is when he noticed—two feet were suspended in mid-air. That is what they had collided with. He gasped and staggered back. Naaz looked up and screamed. She scrambled on her fours to get away from what she had just seen. She was hyper-ventilating. Shirish held up the fire torch to light up what was in front of them. The glow slowly lit up the object with which they had collided.

The light from the fire torch exposed the body . . . and then the face . . .

Naaz shrieked.

Rafique was staring back at them with a grotesque expression of surprise. His mouth was open, and his tongue was hanging out. His body was hanging from the wooden rafters of the roof. But his eyes were wide open—staring back at them.

Both Shirish and Naaz were taken by surprise as they stumbled back in shock.

"Fuck! Fuck!" was all Shirish could say. After a minute when his head began to clear, with a quaking voice Shirish suggested, "We have to get him down." He could not believe what he was seeing.

"Hold his legs. I am going to burn the rope," Shirish tried reaching the rope with the fire torch, trying to burn it.

Naaz stood there watching, hesitant to touch Rafique's body.

"Naaz! He is dead! He is not going to do anything to you! It's just a body! Please hold his legs or he is going to fall," Shirish commanded Naaz, who was in a stupor. She walked up and gingerly held Rafique's legs. She was petrified.

She looked up to see Rafique, and gasped! He was staring at her with his grotesque frozen expression of death. She quickly looked away and shut her eyes. The rope burnt through the rope, and Rafique's corpse came down in a split second. Naaz couldn't take the weight, and she collapsed as she let Rafique's corpse fall. His head hit the cold cement floor. A slow stream of blood trickled out from under his head. Rafique continued to stare at them.

"We need to take his body with us!" Shirish felt he was stuck inside a nightmare.

Immediately a whisper brushed through the silence . . .

"He stays here . . ."

Goosebumps broke out on the surface of their skin. They looked around but found nobody.

"Shirish, let's go from here. Let's find the others and get out of this place!" Naaz pleaded through her sobs.

"Fuck!" Shirish cursed under his breath, took Naaz by her hand, and headed off to find Sneha and Raghav.

Just as they turned around the corner, they bumped into Raghav who was out of breath. As soon as Raghav saw Naaz and Shirish, he broke down and hugged them. And in between sobs told them what he had just witnessed.

"Rafique is dead," Naaz whispered, as if her own voice was unwilling to fathom and comprehend the reality.

"Somebody . . . or something killed him," Shirish was broken. He was scared.

"We need to find Sneha—we have to find her before it is too late," Raghav wiped his tears away. A sudden determination had seeped into his mind.

They all ran toward the church.

The church was ruined and boarded up. The naked bulb hanging from the covered entrance emitted a dull glow, around which insects danced, comforted by the warmth, hypnotized by the glow, and yet too hot to touch.

"Sneha! Sneha!" They all called out.

They now walked toward the graveyard. Most of the graves had tombstones that were worn away.

"There she is!" Neha screamed. The flames from the torches revealed Sneha seated on a grave.

"Sneha! Sneha! Are you okay?" Naaz ran toward her friend, and then she suddenly stopped in her tracks.

Sneha's expression of fear and terror was now frozen on her face. Her mouth opened in a silent scream that had been stifled. Her eyes staring into the infinite distance.

Naaz stifled a sob. Raghav and Shirish slowly lifted Sneha's corpse off the grave and laid her down on the grass.

The sky was enveloped in an amber hue. The sounds of

the chirping of birds returned to flood the trees. It was as if the pall of despair and doom had been lifted with the emergence of daylight.

The three of them looked at each other. They were dishevelled, their faces and clothes streaked with grime. They looked like they had survived a war. They hugged each other and broke down.

****

The Lohaghat police station registered a case of suicide for Rafique and continued to investigate the death of Sneha, at least on paper.

Access to the Abbott Mount Hospital and church was shut down for a few years. Of late ghost-hunters and video bloggers have reignited the curiosity and the mystery behind the place through their videos on social media.

Shirish and Naaz broke up a few months later. Naaz joined a college in Delhi University, New Delhi, and stayed at her uncle's place.

Shirish and Raghav finished their college and went their separate ways.

That one night of adventure led to two deaths.

But it just wasn't them that were affected. Something also died within the other three.

Abbott Mount continues to intrigue people. It has been bought over by a businessman and no sightings or reports have emerged of the place being haunted.

****

THE EXQUISITE HOTEL*

There is a British-era hotel in the hill station, Mussoorie. Built in English Gothic architecture style mostly in wood, the hotel is spread over many acres and overlooking the Himalayas.

The Hotel has had a very rich history with royal families, dignitaries, and aristocrats staying here. But there have also been mysterious deaths associated with the hotel, including that of a clairvoyant Lady Mitchell**.

---

*   The name of the hotel has been changed for legal reasons.
**   The name of the person has been changed for legal reasons.

THE TIME
KEEPER

2008

It was a long-awaited honeymoon for the Kulkarnis. The closest hill station that both of them had ever been to, in their lives, had been Panchgani and Mahabaleshwar. Mussoorie was on their bucket list since they had gotten married. With corporate jobs, both had found it tough to synchronize their annual leave and Pushkar being a workaholic always seemed to be 'busy' or had some 'important client meeting' coming up. Shweta had to really sulk, scold, cajole, seduce, and even threaten Pushkar to apply for his leave.

"I swear, if you don't take me out this winter you will be in serious trouble," she had threatened him. What followed was a month of Pushkar speaking with his boss Dev, who of course found ways to keep giving him more work, and like every toxic corporate sector boss, made it seem that utilizing one's rightful leave, was illegal, unnecessary, and wasteful.

"How will your department run with you gone for a week?" Dev had asked accusingly.

"Sir, there are eight other people in the department! I will finish my work, I assure you!" Pushkar had pleaded.

"What if some important client meeting pops up, or a pitch?" Mita who was his wife and the CFO of the company returned the ball across the net.

"But that can happen any time of the year—so do I not go on leave, on the possibility that a client MIGHT pop in?" Pushkar returned the ball.

"Why can't you take your work with you on your holiday—you know enjoy the holiday and keep working as well?" Dev tried his luck. Pushkar stared at Dev with incredulity. This would have been construed as a bad joke with anyone else, but with Dev it was serious.

"After all we will be paying you salary for the days that you are on leave . . ." Mita trailed off. She too was in the habit of making mandatory 'leave' sound akin to shirking work.

In his mind, Pushkar abused Dev and his wife Mita the two people who over the years, had effortlessly created a toxic work environment, exploiting employees and treating them like bonded slaves.

Pushkar reminded his boss, "But sir, you went on a 28-day leave two months ago with ma'am! And the department ran just fine!"

Pushkar had thought that he finally had Dev against the wall.

"But that's because you were here . . ." Dev smashed the ball, "That's why it's important for you to be around."

And this verbal tennis match continued with ifs, buts, maybe, but why . . .

Finally Dev had to give in and sanction Pushkar's leave. Just as Pushkar was stepping out of the cabin, Dev asked "So where are you going on your vacation?"

"Sir, Mussoorie."

"But why so far? Go to Lonavala, Panchgani—somewhere close by—so that if there is an emergency I can call you back or send you the documents!"

In his head, Pushkar flipped the finger at his boss and said a 'fuck you', but aloud he said, "Sir you went to the UK, for 28 days—did we send you any mails, or bother you? No. So I have also told my department not to bother me for a week."

Pushkar walked out with a scowl on his face.

Prick. Asshole. *Gandu.* Words floated in his head.

"He tries to make me feel guilty every year when I apply for leave!" Pushkar's anger still hadn't calmed down when he returned home!

"But all corporate bosses are like that. They make it seem like work is life and there is nothing beyond that. It's modern-day slavery Pushu!" Shweta hugged her husband and gave him a peck on his cheek.

"Chalo, have a shower and come for dinner! Shanti has made biryani today!"

Shanti was their cook and help who had the keys to their house. Like many Mumbai houses, where both husband and wife are working, they had handed over the house keys to the

115

maid who came in at her convenient time to do her chores. Of course this trust came after many years of working in their house and then they had taken all the personal details of Shanti, before arriving at this mutually beneficial arrangement.

Shanti said that she was from West Bengal. But Shweta knew that Shanti was actually a Bangladeshi illegal immigrant who had entered India a few years ago and had managed to get hold of a ration card and an Aadhar card and had become a legal Indian.

'It's a life about survival. Everybody has to do something to keep their stomachs filled' was the way Shweta had justified it in her head.

So the Kulkarnis flew from Mumbai to New Delhi and then took a private taxi to Mussoorie. The drive up took them six hours and then some more. They alighted from the car in the hotel's driveway. Shweta gasped. Pushkar stretched himself.

In front of them stood a castle-like structure with beautiful green turrets and expanses of green lawns. The evening sun cast a golden glow on the structure, giving it an otherworldly feel.

"It is even more beautiful than the photos!" she exclaimed. They strolled up the steps, then passed by an ornate fountain. As they walked under the wooden archways of the main door—they could feel an excitement rush through their veins.

The Kulkarnis checked into The Exquisite. It was a plush five-star hotel with a grand lobby.

"So is this hotel . . ." Before Pushkar could even complete his question, the receptionist replied, "No sir, the hotel is not haunted. It used to be a colonial hotel. The hotel is slated to get a makeover soon. There is a large corporate house that will be buying the property. Yours is one of the final bookings that we accepted before we shut down. When I was growing up a kid in Mussoorie, we too were told a lot of stories about the hotel. You know how it is with old structures. People just expect them to have a spooky past."

"How old is this hotel?" Shweta asked as she handed over her ID card to be photocopied.

"It was built in the 1900s by Colin Lancashire, an English lawyer from Calcutta. You will see a lot of old photographs on the walls. They are quite interesting," the receptionist rattled off the facts *ad nauseam*. He had to deal with the same question with every guest.

"Oh so you were quite looking forward to some ghostly visits, is it?" Shweta teased Pushkar.

"I am afraid you are going to be disappointed," the receptionist smiled and handed their room key to the bellboy.

As they walked toward the room, the Kulkarnis took in the grand décor. Shweta walked with her arm entwined with Pushkar's. She leaned into him.

"It's beautiful! It's like being a part of history!"

"I couldn't help but overhear your conversation with the receptionist," the bellboy spoke up. Pushkar checked his nametag—Manoj.

"So Manoj, you have the habit of eavesdropping?" Pushkar joked.

"No, no sir! I just heard you speak with him. And every other guest always has the same question. If you really want to know about the hotel's past and hear about the ghost stories, you might want to visit the Old Landour Market and speak with Sharmaji. His name is Avduth Sharma and he runs a curio shop. You can ask anyone there for his shop, and they will show you."

"Maybe we will!" Shweta said.

The room was luxurious and had everything including the most important commodity that a city born and bred traveler needed—free Wi-Fi! By the time they freshened up, the sun had set. Pushkar pulled Shweta onto the luxurious four-posted bed.

"What can I do for you, your Majesty?" she teased.

"As the consort, maybe you can start off by giving me a kiss!"

"Consort? You demoted me just because you are now lying down on this royal bed?" Shweta hit him playfully on his chest. He grabbed her hands and pulled her toward him. She fell on him. Their faces were inches apart. A beat. And then Pushkar pulled her face to his and kissed her. His hands traveled across her back trying to find the clasp of the salwar. Her hands navigated through the gaps between the buttons on his shirt. She pulled away for an instant and removed her salwar. Pushkar stared like a love-lorn teenager. He never got tired of seeing her. His fingers traced the curve of her breast. Shweta elicited a gasp and closed her eyes. Pushkar sat up, buried his head in her bosom and inhaled.

A crash! Shweta shrieked in panic. They were startled and looked around. A framed photograph had fallen off the wall. The glass was broken, leaving shards on the wooden floorboards.

"Fuck! Did it have to fall now?" Pushkar complained and then he tried to pull her back. Shweta broke away saying, "Wait. We have to get this mess cleaned up, or one of us is going to step on the shards at night!"

The boy from room service arrived and began cleaning up the mess. He examined the rope at the back of the photo frame which had held it up.

"This rope looks old. Must have aged and frayed over the

years. So sorry about this," the boy swept the glass shards into a dustpan.

"Whose portrait is it?"

"This is the picture of Mr. Colin Lancashire. He built this hotel," the boy replied. He took one more look at the carpet to ensure that no shards of glass remained. "Sir dinner will be served at 7.00 p.m. in the dining hall," saying this he excused himself and exited.

At 7.00 p.m. they walked into the dining hall. It had a large ceiling with wooden panelling. A chandelier that must have seen better days hung from the ceiling. There were very few people in the dining room. Most of them were foreigners. The *maître d'* showed them their table. The air smelt of food, fungus, and a wet dog.

"I hope the food is not as smelly as the carpet," Pushkar joked.

"Look there's an old grand piano in the corner," Shweta exclaimed, "Maybe you can play it."

Pushkar's parents had forced him to take up piano lessons as a child. He hated it. He loved music, but he hated doing the scales. He hated the tutor forcing his fingers to land correctly on the correct keys.

"Why can't I play with any finger that I want?" the eight-year-old Pushkar had complained.

"Can you play cricket with a hockey stick?" his tutor Mrs. Susan Murray had asked, towering over him. Her gold-rimmed spectacles threatened to slip off her nose, only being held back by the gold chain dangling around her neck.

"We play it with a ruler at school," Pushkar had piped back. His reply was met with a loud "harrumph!" as Mrs. Murray proceeded to place his fingers in the correct position.

"The piano is broken. Only a few strings survive," the waiter said as he served them the food.

"That saves me from revisiting a nightmare," Pushkar joked.

The dinner, a four-course one cheered them up as they tucked in.

"I'll just take a walk, smoke a cigarette, and then I will join you," Pushkar felt the pangs triggered by nicotine depletion.

"Such fresh mountain air and you are going to pollute that!" Shweta disapproved of his smoking and had been trying to get him to give it up but to no avail. She went off to her room.

The corridor was empty. It was dimly-lit with huge portraits hung on the walls, interspersed with smaller frames that captured historical moments connected to the hotel. The temperature had definitely dipped. Pushkar rubbed his palms together and blew into his hand to generate some warmth. He then took a walk toward the open lawns of the hotel.

Crickets and an occasional hoot of an owl in the distance. He sat down on one of the benches facing the hotel. The façade of the hotel was lit up, but now in the dim yellow lights, it seemed like an old lady, past her youth, struggling to sit up straight. He fished out his cigarette and put one to his mouth. Pushkar realized that he didn't have a lighter. He had surrendered it at the airport security. And the box of matches that he had borrowed from the driver had been left in the pocket of his jeans. He cursed under his breath. He really needed to smoke. He looked around to see if there were any hotel staff around or even a security guard. But there were none. He was about to put the cigarette back into its box, when a click was heard, and a flame was in the front of his face.

Pushkar almost jumped up in surprise. He looked up to see a Caucasian lady, probably in her fifties holding up a silver lighter in front of his face.

"I thought you could do with a little flame," the lady spoke with a perfect British accent.

Pushkar thanked her, as he lit his cigarette. He noticed that she was dressed in an elegant formal evening gown and wore a pearl necklace with matching pearl earrings. She took out a cigarette holder, placed her cigarette in it, and then lit it. Her gloved hands with the cigarette holder looked rather regal and posh, Pushkar thought to himself.

"Just arrived today?" she asked. Pushkar nodded.

"Lovely. It is a beautiful place," she said.

By the way I am Pushkar from Mumbai," Pushkar looked at her and smiled, "I feel rather under-dressed seeing you in your beautiful gown."

The lady laughed.

"Just an old habit—dressing up for dinner. I am from England," saying this pulled the trail of her dress, getting ready to leave. "Nice to meet you Pooshkaar (sic). I guess I will be seeing you around."

"We are here for a week," Pushkar replied.

"I am going to be here much longer than that," she said, smiled, and outstretched her hand to shake Pushkar's hand.

As he watched her walk away across the lawn toward the hotel, the clouds moved in to slowly cover the moon. Darkness enveloped the night. Pushkar shivered and decided to go back inside.

Puskar retraced his footsteps to the entrance of the dining hall. The room was dark, except for the center of the room which was dimly flooded by the light from the ancient chandelier. Pushkar tiptoed in. He didn't know why he was there. He had just suddenly found himself at the door. He stood in the center of the room. His body bathed in the warm glow from the chandelier, which made him look like he was being beamed up in an episode of Star Trek.

*Suddenly, he heard a giggle. He swivelled around trying to find the source. There was darkness all around him.

Silence.

Silence.

Silence. He could hear himself breathing. He realized that his heartbeat had gone up exponentially.

Silence.

The piano played four notes in the third octave.

Db Eb - silence - followed by G A

Pushkar's piano theory lessons came back to him. He recognized the notes. He had to undertake many blindfolded lessons as a child. Mrs. Murray would play notes and chords while the blindfolded Pushkar had to correctly identify them. A mistake meant a rap on the knuckles with her wooden ruler.

Pushkar turned toward the piano in the dining hall.

---

* If you want to read along the following portion that's marked in bold with its own background music, then scan the QR Code to access the music and get ready to immerse yourself in the story.

Hadn't the waiter said only a few strings survived? How could it be pitch-perfect and in tune?

A lamp near the piano slowly faded up. Pushkar could now see a man dressed in a suit playing the piano with his back toward Pushkar.

Db Eb - silence - followed by G A
Db Eb - silence - followed by G A

"Hello?" Pushkar's voice was barely audible. *Who was playing the piano so late at night in the darkened dining hall?* He started walking slowly toward the piano. With his every step, the keys played in tempo as if providing ominous background music to the scene.

Db Eb - silence - followed by G A
Db Eb - silence - followed by G A

"Hello?" Pushkar said again, hoping to grab the attention of the pianist. He realized that it was an old man seated at the piano from his white shoulder-length hair. The pianist kept playing the four notes repeatedly on a loop.

Suddenly, the man turned around, just as Pushkar was three feet away from him.

Pushkar's scream was caught in his throat as he looked at what was staring back at him.

The man was decrepit, and all that remained intact was his hair. Where there should have been eyes, were hollow eye sockets. The skin from his face had peeled off exposing bits of the bones

underneath. The old man smiled a grin with his semi-rotten lips and said, "Have you come to join us for the dance?"

Pushkar could not reply as he tried to speak.

The old ghoul laughed out loud. The chandelier flickered. Pushkar was finding it hard to breathe. He tried to suck in a lungful of air in a desperate attempt to stay alive . . .

With a scream, he woke up. Shweta immediately sat up and tried to make him comfortable by stroking his back.

"What happened?" she asked in a panic.

Pushkar couldn't speak. He was still gasping for air.

"I have told you so many times to give up smoking! It's not good for your sleep apnea!"

Pushkar slowly calmed down and tried to recollect what he had dreamed.

Was it a dream? It had felt so real. The smell of the dining room, the sounds of the piano and the flickering chandelier, the old man and his laughter still reverberated in his head . . . or maybe it was the dinner and bad digestion . . . or maybe it was his sleep apnea . . . his head seemed to be enveloped in a fog.

In the morning, Pushkar tried to forget the strange incident and decided distraction was the remedy.

"I am alright. I am okay," he finally spoke, "Let's go and do some sightseeing. I need some fresh air."

They hired an Innova to take them around. Pushkar seemed to cheer up as he felt the cold breeze caress his face as they drove toward Mindrolling Monastery located at Dehradun's Clement Town, a two-hour drive from The Exquisite.

Shweta fell in love with the monastery. It was grand and beautiful and yet so spiritual.

They next headed to Sahastradhara—a series of small waterfalls across the Baldi River, rich in sulfur. They traveled on the ropeway to get a scenic view of the waterfalls and the entire city. Everything seemed normal and happy. On the way back they decided to visit the Old Landour market.

As they walked through the market they took into the old-world charm of the shops. It was a narrow road just wide enough for a car and motorbike to pass through. There were shops selling vegetables, sweetmeats, curios, handicrafts, general stores . . . and that is when Pushkar had the brainwave.

"Hey Shweta remember what Manoj at the hotel had told us? We should meet Sharmaji and find out more about the hotel."

"What's there to find out? It's a hotel that's old and now soon going to shut down," then she realized why Pushkar had thrown up the idea, "Don't tell me you are still curious about the ghost stories?"

Seeing Pushkar smile, she just shook her head, "Are you serious?"

"You can pick up some curios from his shop, while I pick up some ghost stories," Pushkar was now eager to meet Avduth Sharma. So off they went and located the old curio shop.

As they pushed open the door a brass bell placed over the door rang out. It was musty. The shelves were overcrowded with items. A smell of metal, carpets, and incense sticks hovered in the air. Avduth Sharma, the 85-year-old, looked up from behind the counter. His thick glasses were bifocals from an earlier era. He greeted them.

"Welcome. Is there anything particular you are looking for?" he said slowly and smiled. He was bald. His pate reflected the lights of the shop.

"Just some curios to take back home as mementos," Pushkar said. Shweta looked around the shop trying to find anything that would strike her as interesting and economical.

"Where are you folks from?"

"Mumbai."

"Aah the city of dreams! It's been a while since I last went there. Let's just say it was so long ago that the city was still called Bombay then," Avduth had a very kind smile.

"I heard yours is one of the oldest shops in the market," Pushkar tried to now slowly steer the conversation toward the old, the ancient, and the myths.

"Yes, started off with my grandfather, and then I took over when I was still in my early twenties. Never looked back. So where are you staying?" he asked.

"The Exquisite. We just checked in yesterday."

At the mention of Exquisite, Pushkar noticed the smile from Avduth's face disappear. It was as if he immediately knew why they had come to his shop.

"If you have come to hear the ghost stories because some bellboy at the hotel recommended my name—I am sorry, you have come to the wrong place. I am quite done telling those stories," Avduth seemed irritated.

"Well, I will be honest. I did come here to find out more about the ghosts of The Exquisite. But if you don't want to talk about it, that's okay," Pushkar looked disappointed. But he knew that he had been caught out by Avduth.

The earnestness and honesty of Pushkar seemed to impress Avduth who softened up, "I am sorry if I sounded rude. But

I am quite done with tourists coming and hearing the stories. Then not believing a word that I said to them and thinking that it's all fun and games and some make-believe urban legend!"

"I do believe in ghosts," Pushkar said, "And I am not here to make fun of you or disbelieve you. I love history."

"Do you think this would look nice on the sitting room wall?" Shweta had picked up a Tibetan demon mask.

Pushkar nodded. He wanted to get back to speaking with Avduth. Shweta made a face and went back to her shopping.

"The Exquisite has a very interesting story about how it became haunted," Avduth began, ready to tell his story to a believer.

"An incident took place here that inspired a novel. It was the death of a Miss Mitchell. She was a 49-year-old spiritualist, who came to visit Mussoorie with her companion Miss Emily Sykes. They stayed at The Exquisite. Emily also happened to be a specialist in seances, planchet, and crystal gazing. Remember in those days, these were looked upon as being taboo, or even ludicrous. So, a day after Miss Sykes went back to Lucknow, Miss Mitchell was found dead in her hotel room, with all the doors and windows locked from inside. There was chaos. An autopsy followed, revealing that she had been poisoned with prussic acid, a cyanide-based poison. Strangely, a month after the murder, even the doctor who did the autopsy was found dead because of the same poisoning within the hotel in a locked room. There was a court case but Emily was found not guilty. But that's not the only mysterious death that has happened at The Exquisite."

Avduth paused to catch his breath. Pushkar looked over his shoulder to see that Shweta too was now rapt with attention, listening to the stories.

"The Exquisite continued to be plagued by mysterious deaths. In 1951, a hotel employee was found hanging inside a vacant room. Five years later another employee, a cleaning lady, was found hanging in another room. Both these cases remained a mystery and were closed by the police as suicides."

"What do you think?" Avduth asked Pushkar.

Pushkar could not speak. His throat felt dry.

"So whose ghost haunts the place?" he asked a bit shakily.

"Quite a few. But the most prominent one is that of Miss Mitchell's ghost."

It was getting late. Pushkar thanked Avduth and paid the bill for the purchases. As they were heading out, Avduth said, "If you do come across any of them, do not panic. They mean no harm." He paused for a few seconds before adding a caveat, "Usually."

The ride back to the hotel was silent. Both Pushkar and Shweta sat in the car and did not know what to say. When they stepped into the hotel, they were on edge. Having heard about the stories, they were now hyper-alert.

That night, after dinner, Pushkar headed out to the bench to have his smoke. He was feeling uneasy. He was just about done, when suddenly he heard the crunch of dried leaves and he turned around to see the foreigner lady standing there. She was wearing the same evening dress that Pushkar had seen her in, last night.

"Aah you gave me quite a fright," he laughed.

"I have heard that one before. But you are probably the only one who is still smiling after that," she said.

"Well, goodnight," Pushkar got up to leave.

"Do you mind walking me back to my room?" the lady asked, "It's quite scary in these old, deserted corridors."

Pushkar being a gentleman agreed.

They walked to her room. The corridor was dimly lit and Pushkar could not see the number on the door.

"Well thank you Pooshkaar. You are quite a gentleman," she smiled and offered her hand to him. On her hand, she wore a silk glove. Pushkar went to shake her hand. Her hand was cold. Pushkar could feel the cold through the glove. She laughed.

"You are supposed to kiss it, not shake it. Ladies don't shake hands. It is considered too forward."

Pushkar was a little embarrassed and he took her hand and kissed the back of it.

She knocked on the door, "By the way I am Mitchell."

When Pushkar heard this, a chill went through his spine. His knees buckled.

And that is when Pushkar started feeling ill. He blacked out.

****

"Ma'am please relax. We will find him," the manager was trying to pacify Shweta. Shweta had fallen asleep as soon as she hit the bed. When she woke up, the Sun was already up and she was surprised to see Pushkar's side of the bed untouched. She had panicked and immediately rushed off to the reception.

The local police officer walked in—Inspector Paritosh Sharma.

Sharma listened to Shweta's story about Pushkar stepping out to smoke and not returning to his room. The constables were sent out to search the property. There were already rumours flying amongst the staff.

"So what are they saying?" Sharma asked Constable Vinod.

"Sir they are saying it is the work of the ghosts who live here," saying this Vinod sniggered and could not control himself any longer, "Sir, *paagal hai ye log! Bhoot-preth hota hai kya?*" (These people are insane. There are no ghosts and spirits).

"Well, if it is not there, we better find a body at least," Sharma joked.

Searching of the grounds led to nothing. They recovered the cigarette butts from near the bench and Shweta identified them as being Pushkar's brand of preference.

The hotel-staff were on edge. Inspector Paritosh Sharma was standing in the warm sunshine on the lawns of the hotel, facing the ancient structure. The manager, Mr. Topno was standing beside him. Topno was a pious man from Bihar. His forefathers were tribals who had been converted to Christianity a couple of hundred years ago. So Topno grew up with a strong belief in all things Christian.

"So what you are telling me, is that there are ghosts in this hotel?" Sharma couldn't believe that he was asking such a question!

Topno nodded his head, "Sir when the souls are not happy, or they have had a traumatic end, they roam around . . ."

The inspector cut him off. "Don't feed me this bullshit Topno."

Sharma was from Allahabad. His family had been staunch supporters of the right wing Sangh. From an early age Sharma had seen his father dress up in khaki shorts and head out to these meetings. When he was eight-year-old, Paritosh was also introduced to the Sangh where he was inculcated with right-wing pro Hindu doctrines which put the Hindu pantheon of Gods and Goddesses above everything else. He was taught that Hindus were always at threat from minorities and that India was only for Hindus.

His education at the Police Academy broadened his horizons and understanding. But there were times, when the bigoted troll in him was triggered. And he spared no opportunity to unleash it upon others.

"Sir, surely you know what Hinduism and the Bhagavad Gita says about ghosts?" Topno asked.

Tiwari was quite taken aback at Topno's response.

Topno was well-educated and liberal. He had majored in Hotel Management and even done his MBA. He was used to being trolled for his dark skin, for his tribal background, his ST/SC status, his faith, and anything and everything that people used against him right from his days at school. So he was not going to get bullied or insulted by Tiwari.

"Enlighten me!" the inspector barked.

"Lord Krishna is said to have told his dearest friend Arjuna in the Bhagavad Gita, 'Those who worship the demigods will take birth among the demigods; those who worship ghosts and spirits will take birth among such beings; those who worship ancestors go to the ancestors; and those who worship Me will live with Me.' So, even Bhagavad Gita has acknowledged the existence of ghosts and spirits." Topno continued, *"bhoot*, in Hindu mythology is said to be a restless ghost. Bhoots are believed to be malignant if they have died a violent death or have been denied funeral rites."

"What abut your Bible—does that mention ghosts and spirits?" Sharma was upset that a Christian fellow seemed to know more about Hinduism and the Bhagavad Gita than him!

Topno smiled, "For instance, in the book of Samuel, Saul consults a medium who brings a spirit of what Saul believes is that of the recently deceased prophet Samuel.

In the Book of Job, Job's friend Eliphaz describes a frightening encounter he had in the middle of the night, when, 'A spirit glided past my face, and the hair on my body stood on end. It stopped, but I could not tell what it was.'

"In Islam, there is the concept of Djinns which are invisible spirits mentioned in the Quran and believed to inhabit the earth and which can appear in the form of humans or animals."

"Sir, in all religions there is the mention of ghosts and spirits, and the paranormal. Just because most of us don't see them, does not mean that they don't exist!"

"Fuck you Topno!" Sharma was now fully triggered. He refused to even understand what Topno was saying. His face was inches away from Topno.

"I will shut your hotel down. I believe the guest was murdered by your hotel staff. I will get to the bottom of it. Don't give me your cock-and-bull story about ghosts!" Saying this Paritosh Sharma stomped away.

Back at the reception, Shweta hounded the inspector for answers.

"We are investigating ma'am. Please have some patience. He is a fully grown man—he just can't disappear into thin air."

****

Pushkar slowly opened his eyes. It took him a while to adjust his eyes to the darkness around him. There was just a chink of sunlight streaming into the room from between the heavy brocade curtains. He sat up on the bed and looked around. And it came back to him. He panicked. He wondered if he was dead.

"You are not dead," a voice said from within the dark corner of the room. Pushkar was petrified. And a figure glided toward his bed. He shrank back when he saw it was Mitchell.

"Who are you? What am I doing here? Where am I?" he asked in panic.

Mitchell slowly tilted her head and listened to the rambling queries from Pushkar. And then she laughed. The laugh sent chills down his spine.

"I am Mitchell. Don't you remember? And you are still at The Exquisite. Where else will you be?"

"But how is that possible? You are the Mitchell who died here?"

"Oh that? Hah! Death is just transitory. I have always lived here. And now so will you."

"I need to leave. I need to get back to my room, to my wife." Pushkar said as he got out of the bed.

"I think that will not be possible," Mitchell said. There was a tinge of threat in her voice.

Pushkar ran to the door and tried to open it. He turned the door knob several times, but the door remained locked.

Mitchell laughed aloud.

"You may keep trying the door but it is not going to open."

Pushkar screamed in panic. He could not comprehend what was going on.

"You must let me go!" saying this Pushkar walked toward Mitchell.

Mitchell screamed a loud 'No' and opened her mouth wide. Black, acrid smoke came out of her mouth like a living entity and smashed against Pushkar. It lifted him off the ground.

Mitchell was no longer the sweet lady that he had met. Her eyes were cavernous pools of black. Her face was a sneer of rage. And she spoke in a voice that was deep and angry.

"You belong to us now. You belong to The Exquisite!"

Saying this Mitchell disappeared right before his eyes. And Pushkar was thrown on the ground.

He curled up in fright and wondered what his fate would be. The logical side to him continuously questioned what he was seeing, and what was happening. How could a ghost communicate with him? How could a ghost keep him captive?

This was a bad dream, perhaps? He was stuck in a nightmare. He looked around. He tried to wake up from the dream. But nothing happened. He was still here. Maybe some mad guest was playing a prank on him? How could Mitchell be so lifelike when she was supposed to be dead a hundred years ago? He got up. He needed to escape. He opened the heavy curtains. The sun hit him squarely in the face, and blinded him for a moment. He looked out and what he saw baffled him.

In the garden lawns of the hotel, outside the room, were two men dressed in long English coat-tails and women in frilly white dresses with parasols walk past the window. He banged the panes of the window but they didn't seem to hear him. He screamed aloud at the top of his lungs and it was as if he was in a vacuum from which no sound escaped.

He ran to the chest of drawers to see if he could find anything to pry open the door with. His eyes fell on a folded newspaper. It looked fresh. He wanted to check and see how many days he had been in this bizarre captivity. He quickly unfolded the newspaper. It wasn't a newspaper he was familiar with. The mast-head read *The Hills*. He checked the date and he seemed to choke up. He staggered, the newspaper slipped from his hand and fell to the ground. The date on the newspaper was 'Friday, 18th November 1910.'

****

2008

Sanjay, the young house-keeping boy, wheeled the dirty laundry down the corridor of the hotel. Even though it was daylight, he still felt scared. He had grown up in Mussoorie hearing the stories of the haunted hotel from his childhood days. He distinctly heard the sound of a doorknob rattling. His heart raced as an icy shiver crawled down his spine. There was no one in the corridor. He cautiously wheeled the laundry cart, telling himself that it was all just his own imagination.

And then again! The rattling of the doorknob. He slowly turned to look at the door on which the doorknob was rattling. His feet seemed to be glued to the floor. It was room 505. He could see the doorknob moving rapidly.

But how was that possible? The room had been completely boarded up years ago . . .

Sanjay abandoned the laundry cart and disappeared, running as fast as he could, to put distance between himself and the cursed room.

Shweta at first had tried to call Pushkar's mobile phone. But she realized that he had left it in the room, when they had stepped out for dinner. She then went through the messages to see if anything untoward had been communicated. No calls from strangers, or even his wretched boss. Shweta was at her wits' end. She screamed in frustration.

****

1910

As Pushkar lay on the carpeted floor, he heard a scream—a faint scream, coming from a distance. This was followed by the sounds of a woman crying. He slowly sat up wondering where the sound was coming from.

A mobile phone rang somewhere. How could a mobile phone exist and ring in 1910? Pushkar thought maybe it had been a prank . . . maybe he wasn't stuck in 1910!

Someone was now speaking over the phone. He could not make out what was being said—it was a muffle. And then he recognized the voice . . . it was Shweta's! Pushkar started running around the room putting his ears to the wall to see where the sound was coming from. He was not in 1910? If he could hear her voice then he was still in 2008! Pushkar located an air vent in the room near the floor. He put his ears close to it—and yes—there it was—Shweta's voice . . . muffled—but clearly identifiable. Pushkar realized that if he could hear her—then she would be able to hear him as well. He put his mouth close to the air vent and screamed her name!

****

2008

"The police are looking for him, ma. We will find him. Maybe he fell off the mountain in the dark," Shweta was trying to be as hopeful as possible. She knew that if she appeared despondent while speaking to Pushkar's mother, it would erase the faintest trace of hope. And just then her ears picked up a voice. Faint, coming from a distance. It sounded like someone called her name. She turned around.

"Ma let me just call you back," saying this she quickly disconnected her call. She called out Pushkar's name.

"Pushkar, is that you? Where are you?"

All she could hear was a muffle coming from somewhere.

****

1910

Pushkar wanted to ensure that it was Shweta. He wanted to make a louder noise. He ran to the porcelain lamp in the room, picked it up and smashed it against the wall.

****

Sanjay was now standing outside 505 with Rahim, the concierge. They distinctly heard a muffled voice coming from behind the door of 505, followed by the sound of something being smashed. Their faces were ashen. They had only heard about the hauntings of The Exquisite. For the first time, they were a witness to it.

"We need to tell Topno sir," Rahim tugged on Sanjay's sleeve and urged him to get away from the door.

****

Shweta ran to Topno and told him that she had heard her husband's voice calling out to her. Topno dismissed her.

"Ma'am we have searched all the rooms. He wasn't there," Topno reasoned.

"Search again!" Shweta screamed.

The other guests around the reception area turned and stared at her. Topno just nodded.

****

1910

Pushkar sat on the floor, with his back against the wall. He did not move a muscle. Miss Mitchell sat opposite him, on the floor. Rocking slowly back and forth, singing some song. Suddenly her eyes bore down on Pushkar.

Pushkar winced. She laughed.

"They are all looking for you!" Mitchell whispered, "But you are out of their reach. You are in our world now. You will live out your life here forever."

****

2008

Sanjay and Rahim walked up to Topno.

"Sir we need to speak with you. Urgently."

"What's the matter?" Topno asked.

"Sir room no. 505. We just saw . . ." Sanjay described what he had seen.

Topno's brow creased into multiple folds of worry.

"Okay, don't tell anybody else. Let me make a phone call."

Topno rushed off to his office. The setting sun cast an

orange glow on his desk. He picked up the land phone and punched in the number. The bell rang thrice before it was picked up.

"Good evening. Reverend Subba this side. Who is this?"

"Good evening Reverend. This is Rajesh Topno from The Exquisite."

"Aah Mr. Topno. I hope all well with you. How can I help?"

Topno told him about the disappearance of the guest and the recent poltergeist sightings in 505.

Reverend Subba had shifted to Mussoorie from Sikkim twenty years ago. He had studied exorcism and held a keen interest in paranormal activities. A few years ago, he had exorcised a local boy and helped him recover from the effects of a possession. News had spread like wildfire and now he was swamped with cases of possession. He redirected almost all of them to neurological experts—the children had fits and epilepsy and the demon had nothing to do with them!

"I will be there in an hour," Reverend Subba sensed that something serious was about to go down.

Topno thought of calling up the inspector, but decided against it. Sharma will not believe a thing even if it happens right before his eyes.

And that is when a fleeting thought raced across his mind . . . what if this was the case of the locked room suicides recurring again?

Reverend Subba reached The Exquisite by the time the sun had set. The lights in the lawn had come to life.

"Should we do it now? Or wait for the guests to fall asleep?" Rev. Subba asked.

"I don't think we should wait. I have a bad feeling about this."

And so Topno, Rev. Subba, Sanjay, Rahim and their head of security Bhupendra Chhetri approached room 505.

This was the same room where Miss Mitchell had been found dead more than a hundred years ago. It had a wooden plank across the door. Topno gave the go ahead. Bhupendra took out a hammer and started breaking the plank.

****

1910

Dull thuds reverberated in the room. Mitchell suddenly seemed alert. She smiled, "They have come for you."

Pushkar looked toward the door. He was going to be rescued from this hell!

Mitchell laughed and sang while rocking back and forth . . .

"Too late. Too late.

The raven has sealed your fate.

Time is a wonder, oh what a blunder

Wait till they walk through that gate!"

Pushkar stood up thinking why was she happy if they were coming to rescue him.

****

2008

The plank came off. Topno took out a bunch of old keys from his pocket. One of the keys had a red tape around the bow or the head of the key. He handed the key to Reverend Subba.

"All of you stand back."

He took out Holy Water and while saying a prayer he sprinkled water on the door in the shape of a cross. Then he blessed the door. He slowly slid in the key and tried to turn it. It refused to budge. The room had been locked since the 1960s.

"We will have to break it down." Rev. Subba said.

Bhupendra and Rahim put all their weight against the door and tried to break it down. They shoved against the door again and again. And it gave way and collapsed.

Pushkar suddenly saw the door fly open. He realized that they had indeed come to rescue him. But why was there a priest? Where was the police?

He saw the horrified reaction on the face of the priest.

Rev. Subba stood at the entrance and a sight greeted him. There was an old lady sitting in the chair and laughing. A man's body was suspended in mid-air above the bed.

Rev. Subba started praying aloud as he marched into the room—he held the cross in front of him like a shield as he threw Holy Water on the apparition of Mitchell.

Pushkar looked at the screaming Mitchell who tried to rise up and attack the priest. But the priest was now standing right above her. There was spittle flying from his mouth as his prayers and incantations got louder and louder.

"You are BANISHED!"

With an ear-splitting scream, the ghost of Mitchell disappeared. The suspended body of the man fell on the bed with a loud bang.

Pushkar was relieved. He turned to the priest and said, "Thank you for rescuing me."

But the priest's attention was somewhere else. He turned to the people standing outside the door, "You better come in now and see . . ."

Pushkar saw the people enter the room and gasp. What were they looking at?

"Where is Shweta? Where is my wife?" he asked them. But nobody paid attention to him. They were all staring at the bed.

"Excuse me, where is my wife?" All this while, Pushkar had assumed that it was Shweta who had orchestrated the rescue operation. *'But why isn't she here?'* he thought.

Pushkar looked toward the bed and immediately shrank back in terror. On the bed was his own body. His head reeled. He screamed. He tried to touch the people in the room. But no one could see him. No one could hear him.

Pushkar realized that he had been dead all along—stuck in a time warp chosen by Mitchell. And now that the illusion was broken, the reality hit him.

Shweta burst into the room. Topno had called up the reception to inform her. Seeing Pushkar's body, she collapsed. Pushkar screamed and cried. He was helpless. The police team came in and examined the body and the room. All the while Pushkar sat on the floor in a corner of the room, knowing that he was now fated to live at The Exquisite forever.

A few weeks after the incident, The Exquisite closed down for renovations as it had been bought off by a huge corporate. The new management destroyed room 505 completely.

Sharma could not comprehend how could a dead body turn up in a closed, boarded room.

The Exquisite of old has now given way to a swanky resort, where the past has been erased forever. The ghosts have left the building.

MUKESH
MILLS
MUMBAI

Mukesh Mills is an abandoned textile mill located in South Mumbai.

The mills were first established by Muljibhi Madhvani, the owner of East African Hardware Ltd. in the 1870s. It was the only mill at the time in the South Bombay (Mumbai) which was built on the Arabian Sea Shore of Colaba Region with its own private dock so that ships and boats could unload the bales of cotton as well as load yards of finished clothing. Later around 1975, the 10-acre property underwent an entire renovation but unfortunately, went out of business within a few years after the renovation. The owners applied to the government seeking permission to shut down but were denied. The Mill was suddenly struck by a tragedy in 1982 when it was forced to close down due to a disastrous fire. In the 90s the mill got a new lease of life when it became a shooting location for Bollywood movies including the iconic song 'Jumma Chumma' (*Hum*) to more recent *Ok Jaanu, Heropanti,* and *Badlapur.* The Mill is said to be haunted by one of the workers who died in the mysterious fire.

THE CURSED MILL

Bhavna Basu closed her eyes and leaned back into the plush leather interiors of her Mercedez Benz as it crawled through the atrocious Mumbai traffic. Her secretary Namit sat in the front passenger seat. He looked at his watch. It was 5.17 p.m. He stared at the traffic ahead of him. He clicked his tongue in exasperation.

"What happened Namit?" Bhavna asked with her eyes still closed.

"The traffic. It's horrible. The shift starts at 7.00 p.m. and we will probably reach late."

"Hmm. Call up the director and inform him," she instructed.

Namit took out his mobile and sent an SMS to 'Manish Director'.

"Ma'am?" Namit asked hesitantly.

"*Bolo*..." Bhavna now opened her eyes and sat up realizing that she was not going to get any sleep.

"Err... how to tell you?" Namit hesitated trying to make up his mind, whether to share the information with Bhavna or not.

"Footage *mat khao*. Tell me," Bhavna was terse.

"The location ma'am where we are shooting for the next two days..." Namit began, "Mukesh Mills. It is known to be haunted."

Bhavna stared at Namit and then burst out laughing.

"Are you scared of ghosts?" Bhavna asked through peals of laughter, "There are no things as ghosts, Namit!"

"Ma'am, many crew members of other films have reported that when they shoot here they experience things..." Before Namit could continue, Bhavna cut in,

"Like *chudails* walking with turned feet?" And started laughing again.

Namit was embarrassed. After all the stories he had heard were all hearsay. He had never experienced any hauntings at the Mills on any of his previous shoots there.

"Namit, this is the third movie that I am filming here. Nothing spooky has ever happened during the previous shoots!" Bhavna didn't believe in ghosts or the paranormal. Born in New Delhi, she was an urban child who had no patience for mumbo-jumbo or the paranormal. As a child, her grandmother often told her to not venture out to the terrace at night with open hair. But Bhavna always laughed it off. And nothing ever happened to her, which strengthened her belief that this was all just 'old women's tales.'

"Yes ma'am nothing has happened before because they were all during the day. People say that Mukesh Mills is a completely new entity during the night." Namit was adamant.

"Stop putting all these nonsense ideas in my head! It is the climax of the film and I need to concentrate. Wake me up when we reach there," saying this Bhavna closed her eyes and tried to sleep.

Namit did not argue his point any further. He knew that he had reached a dead end. He just prayed in his head. Namit's cousin sister had committed suicide when she was 17 and Namit often felt her presence every time he went back to his ancestral home in Barabanki. The room where she had hung herself still gave him the chills. He had told his elder brother Sumit about his trepidation at which Sumit had laughed out aloud.

"*Kitna darpok hai tu!* (You are such a scaredy-cat!) Nita's ghost does not roam in the *angan* nor does it reside in that room! It's just your fertile imagination!"

Namit had not retaliated. He knew what he knew—it was a gut feeling. A very strong one. As the car now inched through Colaba and past Café Leopold, Namit quickly said a prayer in his head. The climax of the film was scheduled to be shot over two night shifts (7.00 p.m. to 7.00 a.m.) and he just wanted the shoot to get completed without any incident.

"Ma'am, we have reached," Namit whispered. Bhavna sat up. Pulled out a small compact mirror from her purse and checked herself in it. She put on her large Sophia Loren-esque sunglasses.

"Let's do this!" She said. Namit got off and opened the door for her. Immediately an assistant wearing a T-shirt that had 'CREW' emblazoned on the back approached the car.

"Welcome ma'am. Let me take you to your vanity van," And she then spoke into her walkie talkie microphone. "Okay everybody tell sir that Bhavna ma'am has arrived. She is headed for make-up."

Bhavna looked all around her as she walked toward the vanity van. The crew was busy setting up lights, the catering department was setting up the evening *naashta* (snacks). The derelict walls of the mill were bathed in an orange hue. The setting sun on the sea across the Mills looked majestic. The stark nature of the location always fascinated Bhavna. And every time she stood at the edge overlooking the Arabian Sea, she wondered what it would have looked like earlier in the century when it was a functioning mill with its own dock.

The vanity was a special one reserved usually for the hero and the heroine. It had a bedroom and a sitting room with two attached toilets. Before leaving, the girl handed Namit a walkie-talkie, "We are on channel 6." Namit clipped the walkie to his belt and clipped the earpiece on.

Bhavna settled into the couch. Namit started unpacking her bags. He took out her coffee machine and plugged it in. He started brewing a fresh pot of coffee for her. Bhavna always carried her own coffee. She hated the diluted and cheap instant coffee served at shoots. She took out the script and started reading it.

"Find out from the AD which scene we are shooting first."

Namit spoke into the walkie, "Hi, Namit here. Bhavna ma'am wants to know which scene are we shooting first?"

There was a crackle, and a male voice came on, "Scene 92. The rescue scene. She can get into her costume and makeup. We will need her only by 10."

Namit relayed the message to his boss.

"If they were going to roll my shot at 10.00 p.m., why did they call me in at 7.00 p.m.? Ridiculous! Give me the coffee."

There was a knock on the door.

"Come in," Namit said as he handed the coffee to Bhavna.

"Ma'am, your costume," The costume department had brought in the police inspector's uniform.

"Ruchi, did you remove the tag that was irritating me?" Bhavna asked.

"Yes ma'am" Ruchi replied as she hung the costume in the cupboard, "Do you want to start your makeup now, or . . ."

"I am not needed till 10. It's no use getting my makeup done now. Maybe in an hour, you can ask makeup *dada* (makeup man) to come in," Bhavna was already feeling exhausted.

She hated waiting between takes and shots. It's the pauses in between that made her irritable and fatigued. This movie had been a difficult one. She was playing a female inspector who was out to nab a child trafficker. She had never played a cop before, and so she had worked on her body language, and shooting skills for the film.

****

Ramesh Dutt, the director, was seated in the director's chair looking at the monitor. He was running out of patience.

"How much more time will it take for the lighting? What the fuck is going on?" he screamed into the cordless microphone.

Immediately this set off a series of voices amongst the light men . . .

"Come on hurry up . . ."

"Get the baby . . ."

"See if the generator has come on . . ."

"Where is the socket?"

It seemed like everybody was asking questions, and none of them had answers.

The shot was a simple one establishing the villain's den where six children had been kept captive. The children were supposed to be crying, begging for their lives, while the villain would mouth some dialogues promising the children a quick route to the afterlife if they didn't shut up. The den was set up on one of the dilapidated floors of the mill. The DOP (Director of Photography) had pumped in HMI lights through the arched window frames and had placed an exhaust fan in front of one of the lights. The shadow of the rotating blades on the wall behind the captive children created an eerie and dramatic effect.

After what seemed an hour, the lighting was finally ready and the actors were brought onto the set, and the ADs started briefing the actors and placing them on the set.

The head spot-boy, Chanchal's walkie came alive.

"Spot! Ramesh sir needs his tea now!" Chanchal immediately rushed off to the kitchen area. This was the first time he was working on a Ramesh Dutt film. And he had quickly learned that Ramesh sir drank copious amounts of tea.

"Sir *ka chai ready hai*?" Chanchal asked.

"Two minutes!" replied the spot boy who was in-charge of making the tea.

"Super! I am just going to relieve myself!" Saying this Chanchal headed far from the crowd to find a desolate place to pee.

There were no chemical toilets for the B crew. The A crew comprising the departments of direction, cinematography, script, costume, and makeup had two vanity vans. The B crew which included light men, sound, spot boys, and crew members who were further down in the food chain had to resort to using the derelict mill when the call of nature arrived.

The sun had set, and portions of the mill that were lifeless were now engulfed in darkness. Just as Chanchal was about to unzip, he heard a voice, *"Abbey, idhar mat muth!"* (Don't pee here!)

Chanchal jumped with a start and looked over his shoulder, and broke into a nervous smile. It was Iqbal, one of the light men who was on his way to the shooting area, shouldering an HMI light.

"Kya darr gaya kya? Phattu!" (You got scared? Loser!) Iqbal laughed.

"This place is bloody spooky!" Chanchal had gotten quite a start hearing the voice.

"Be careful, don't venture further! Who knows what the darkness is hiding? This place is haunted!" Iqbal teased, laughed, and vanished with his load.

The distant din from the shooting area floated up to Chanchal. He looked in front of him. There was a tunnel-like structure, beyond which was pure darkness. He shook his head and smiled to himself. Chanchal walked past the tunnel. He unzipped and started relieving himself.

In the pitch darkness something moved. Chanchal immediately stopped peeing. He held on before opening his faucet again. Again, he distinctly heard a rustle. He was not yet done. Another rustle, as if someone or something was taking steps toward him. Chanchal slowly turned his head to look at the direction of the sound. And as he stared, he could clearly see the silhouette of a man standing there watching him. Chanchal's throat suddenly felt parched. His feet were rooted to the spot. His eyes were locked onto the silhouette. Thoughts rushed through Chanchal's mind—*Is it my imagination? It must be another crew member who had probably gone there to relieve himself!*

Chanchal gathered up his courage and asked in a voice that struggled to come out of his larynx, *"Kaun hai wahan?"* (Who's there?). He had hoped that the crew member would step out of the darkness and end his ordeal. But nothing happened. The shadowy figure darted off and melted into the darkness. Chanchal zipped up. He was bathed in a pool of sweat. He ran toward the lights of the shooting area.

****

Smriti, the child actor, was loitering around the mill, even though her parents had asked her to stay put in her designated vanity van. The sun was just setting and she stood at the edge of the mill overlooking the vast expanse of the Arabian Sea stretched out in front of her. On her right, across a narrow canal was the huge fish-market of Bhaucha Dhakka (Brother's Ferry Wharf).

There was a cool breeze blowing in from the sea which ruffled her shoulder-length hair. She had always wanted to be an actress since she was three-years-old. Smriti's parents soon discovered their daughter's knack for acting and recitation. She turned into another person when she was on stage. And so they decided to test the waters. Numerous auditions followed. It was only after six months of their trudging across to various production houses and casting agencies in Aram Nagar that

Smriti got her first break. It was a commercial for ice cream. And luckily, the television advertisement became popular and Smriti soon found herself being cast in movies and television serials. And that is how Ramesh Dutt discovered this ten-year-old girl and cast her in this movie.

She skipped off from the edge back into the mill area. She trailed her hand across the moss-covered broken walls. She walked through a narrow corridor and entered a huge flat open area surrounded by high walls, the tips of which were shaped like triangles. She gasped as she remembered where she had seen this place before. She smiled as she remembered the music video of her favorite song 'Chandu Ke Chacha' by a band called Aasma that was filmed here.

She stood all alone in that quadrangle imitating the dance steps of the song. Her voice echoed in the empty vastness. And that is when she heard a voice. She stopped singing mid-sentence and looked around. '*Maybe, they are calling me for the shot,*' she thought to herself. She looked all around her—there was no one. She walked slowly, looking around and trying to find the shortest exit to the shooting area.

Suddenly, she felt alone. The joy that she had been feeling just a moment ago had been sucked out of her. She felt an empty pit in her stomach. She started walking faster. She entered the corridor like structure. She stumbled as her feet hit debris on the floor. A giggle was heard somewhere behind her. She picked herself up and now started running. She could hear footsteps behind her. And suddenly she felt a hand on her shoulder and she turned around—a scream frozen in her throat.

****

"Okay Smriti, when I say action, you will say your dialogues. You are begging for your life as the goons are tying you up. Makeup, give her glycerine. Let the tears come while you are saying the dialogue. And only start speaking once the camera comes to a halt. Okay, going for take," Ramesh Dutt was ready to shoot.

"Silence on the set," the second AD shouted.

"Roll Sound. Roll Camera," Ramesh gave instructions as he stared closely at the small monitor in front of him.

"Rolling," the DOP said.

"Rolling," the sound recordist replied.

"Scene 89. Take 1," saying this the clapper boy 'clapped' and exited the frame rapidly.

"And . . . Action!" Ramesh Dutt instructed.

The camera was placed on a track and trolley. It started to move slowly toward the captive children, pushed by two attendants. The camera came to a halt. Ramesh watched Smriti in a mid-shot looking off camera, as the goons were tying her with rope to a pillar.

Suddenly, Smriti's head jerked to face the camera. She let out a snarl. Nobody moved. Everybody was too shocked to say anything. Smriti growled as she tugged on the ropes wound around her torso. Effortlessly, they came loose. She gave a low growl. Her eyes were blood-shot as she stared menacingly toward the camera.

Ramesh watched in shock at the scene unfolding in front of him. He came to his senses and yelled, "Cut! Smriti, what happened beta? What are you doing?"

Smriti just cocked her head, watching the director. A low growl emanated from her as her lips formed a macabre smile.

There was pin-drop silence on the set. No one knew what was going on, and therefore how to react. Never in their lives had they seen something as scary and bizarre as this.

Suddenly Smriti got down on her fours and accompanied by a loud scream, she charged toward the cameraman like a feral child.

The DOP screamed and jumped off the track-trolley platform. Smriti looked around the crowd and hissed. The crew members stepped back. The other children who were part of the scene started crying in fright. Their parents quickly grabbed them, in case Smriti decided to turn against them.

Suddenly, Smriti's body twisted and contorted into unimaginable postures. She screamed and then collapsed on the floor. There was silence.

Smriti's parents who were watching in stunned silence rushed and picked up their daughter. Immediately there was commotion amongst the crew members. Some of them helped carry Smriti into her vanity van.

"Production—call a doctor!" an AD yelled.

"I told you this place was haunted!" Iqbal whispered to Chanchal.

A murmur rushed through the crowd like a wave—the ghost of Mukesh Mills was back. The legend had been proven to be true.

The DOP sat with his head in his hands.

Ramesh Dutt looked at his Chief AD, "What the fuck just happened?"

The AD was a rational guy who had already summed up the situation and had come to his own logical conclusion, "Sir, I think she had some kind of fit."

"Fits? Did that look like fits? And we have been filming with her for the past few months—it has never happened before. Go and check on her. If she is unwell, tell her to take rest. We will film the other scenes."

****

Bhavna heard the commotion from inside her vanity van. She parted the curtains of the windows and looked out. There seemed to be more than usual activity. She called up Namit on his phone.

"Namit, has something happened?"

"Ma'am that little girl Smriti. I think she had a fit or something during the take," Namit shared the 'logical' story rather than the one he actually believed in. He did not want to be reprimanded again.

"I hope she is okay. Please check up on her."

"Ma'am you need to get ready as they have preponed (*sic*) your shots. They will do your close ups till the little girl recovers," Namit informed her and rushed off to check on Smriti.

The makeup dada and the hair stylist came in to help Bhavna get ready.

Santosh Bendre was Bhavna's makeup man from her first film. She loved his work. And Santosh liked Bhavna's work ethics.

"Dada, has a doctor visited Smriti for her fits?" She asked as dada applied foundation to her face.

"Fits? Who told you fits? The girl was possessed by the evil spirit," Santosh dada whispered.

Bhavna looked at dada's reflection in the mirror, and then burst out laughing, "*Kya dada, aap bhi?* You will now also tell me this place is haunted?"

Santosh smiled gently, "Ma'am—yes this place is haunted since the mysterious fire happened. One of the factory workers died and his spirit still haunts the place at night."

"Dada, you really believe in this rumor that the place is haunted?" Bhavna was surprised that a man like Santosh dada, who was a man of the world believed in such tripe.

"I have been coming here for shoots since the 90s. I never liked this place. There is something here. Many of us can feel it in our bones! About two years ago, I was here shooting here for an ad. It was a night shoot. I got chatting with the watchman of this place. He told me what he experienced." Santosh went about his story while applying makeup on Bhavna. He checked a photograph of Bhavna's character that he carried, to ensure that he maintained a continuity of her look throughout the film. He checked to see the position of the fake scar. He got some make up glue and pasted the fake scar on the right side of her forehead, as per continuity.

"One night, the watchman was closing the gates of the mill. There were no scheduled shoots that night. So the mill was completely empty. As he was closing the gates, he heard music coming from the inside the mill."

Bhavna interjected, "But sound travels, na Dada? In the dead silent night, somebody in the fish market must have been playing some music and the sound traveled, no?"

Santosh dada smiled and continued, "You are right. But how do you explain this?" And Santosh dada now got ready to serve the punchline.

"When the watchman hearing the music, peeped in to see if there was anybody there by mistake, he spotted a man at a distance standing and smoking. The red light of the cigarette glowed in the dark. The watchman screamed asking the man to come out of the mill. The man suddenly disappeared. The watchman was petrified. He quickly locked up and left, completely shaken up by the incident."

Bhavna could think of many explanations for what she had just heard. Maybe it was some errant man who wanted to hide in the mill for whatever reason . . . or maybe some prankster had come in from Bhaucha Dhakka and climbed up the walls to the mill . . . She did not want to argue with Santosh dada.

"Well, I don't believe in ghosts dada. *Yeh sab bakwaas hai* (It's all rubbish). But it sure is a good story!"

Santosh dada laughed, "Yes, for non-believers like you it is a good story for sure. I don't blame you. Your entire life has been spent in big cities. For people like us who have lived in villages, and have seen many things—this cannot be brushed off as a good story. And since the fire in 1982, this place has been cursed."

Bhavna got ready for her shot and headed to the location accompanied by Namit and an AD who spoke into her walkie alerting everyone on set that Bhavna was headed there.

The pathway leading to the area where the filming was taking place was dark. It was the main road that was in between two rows of what was once thriving factory floors. Now they stood like skeletons.

Ramesh Dutt got up and hugged Bhavna, "Come, take a seat."

A chair was pulled up for Bhavna beside Ramesh Dutt's chair.

Before he could start briefing her on the scene, she started, "I just heard that the little girl has fallen ill."

Ramesh thought carefully about what he was about to say.

"Bhavna, in my 58 years of existence I have not seen anything like this. It didn't look like someone falling ill." Ramesh still looked shaken.

"Come on! Makeup dada said she was possessed by some evil spirit that lurks around here," Bhavna made quotation marks with her fingers for 'evil spirit' reducing the story to a mere rumor. She laughed out loud.

Some of the crew members who had been witness to Smriti's possession, now looked at Bhavna praying that she does not say anything offensive lest the spirit makes his presence on the set again.

Ramesh took Bhavna's hand in his. Bhavna noticed that his hands were shaking.

"Are you okay?" she asked with genuine concern. Ramesh Dutt was the *enfant-terrible* of the movie industry known for his path-breaking movies that weren't coy. *He is known as a tough guy,* Bhavna thought to herself as she held his shaking hand, *what has happened to him?*

Ramesh leaned forward in his chair and looked Bhavna straight in the eyes and spoke slowly, "Have you seen the movie *Exorcist?*"

Bhavna remembered seeing it when she was in college and getting completely freaked out.

"Yes, of course."

"Well, it looked like the movie. It was as if Smriti was possessed, just like Regan was in the movie. The same expressions, the same low growl, the same aggressiveness."

Bhavna who had been skeptical so far, suddenly found that his hands were cold. Her mind was in a turmoil . . . the rational side of her refused to believe it. On the other hand, now that it came from Ramesh Dutt, a man whom she respected and revered, she was forced to look at it differently.

She looked around, as if expecting to see the ghost.

"You mean . . . this place . . . is really haunted? Like with a real ghost?" Bhavna kept trying to rationalize and come to terms with all the information in her head.

"Well, I am a believer now," Ramesh lit a cigarette and took a long drag. He let out the smoke with a leisurely exhale; letting go of all things rational.

"Is the lighting ready?" Ramesh yelled to no one in particular, as happens on any film set, but the message always inevitably reaches the one who has the answer.

Ramesh's query unleashed a flurry of echoes . . .

"Is the lighting ready? The director is asking."

"How long will it take?"

"Where is the gaffer?"

And after 30 seconds, the DOP appeared and gave the answer, "Yes, it is ready."

Ramesh looked at, Shantanu, the DOP, "You are okay? You will manage?"

Shantanu nodded. He still couldn't get the image of Smriti out of his mind. What he saw through the viewfinder had shaken him up. More so, when she had charged at him like a ferocious, wounded animal!

"Come," saying this Ramesh led Bhavna inside a portion of the mill. This was a room adjoining the villain's den.

"So, this is the climax. You have just received the tip-off about the children's whereabouts and you have landed here. The villain hears your voice first. So you will start walking from this room to the next while speaking. It's a long monologue. I hope you have rehearsed it." Ramesh briefed Bhavna.

160

"Yes, sir."

"Great let's go for a rehearsal" Ramesh announced as he headed back to his chair and the monitor.

Instructions were yelled out and Ramesh said "Action" . . .

Bhavna began walking slowly. Her police boots with the metal plating under the heel emanated rhythmic foot-steps that echoed off the walls of the empty factory floor.

Within two lines of her dialogue delivery, Bhavna fumbled. She could not remember her lines, even though she had rehearsed them at home umpteen number of times.

CUT!

"What happened?" Ramesh spoke on the microphone.

"Nothing, sir. I will get it." Bhavna replied looking over her shoulder at Ramesh who was seated outside the structure, at least 30 feet away.

She looked around her. The walls were covered in moss, plants, and black soot.

She remembered Santosh dada mentioning the fire. She wondered if the charred walls were the remnants of the fire of 1982.

"Awesome! Let's go for a take!" Ramesh instructed. Bhavna came out of her reverie and began to focus on her lines. The camera began rolling, the spools on the Nagra recorder began winding, the clapper board exited the frame.

Bhavna began walking and delivering her dialogues and exactly two lines later she fumbled. She tried hard to remember, but she just couldn't say her lines! The shooting halted. Bhavna asked for some water.

Namit walked up to her, "Are you okay? Do you want to rehearse the lines again?"

Bhavna glared at Namit, "I know my lines!" Her anger was

in retaliation of her own helplessness of finding herself locked in this strange experience.

She just could not remember her lines! It was as if she suddenly lost the ability to speak or think.

"Going for another take," the Chief AD announced.

Bhavna, stood all alone in the middle of the empty factory floor. She felt as if she was being watched. She looked down at her feet. And she could swear that the floor was burning! The floor was bathed in an orange glow where she was standing. She shrieked and jumped back.

Pandemonium ensued. Ramesh ran in to see. ADs rushed in. The light men had the fear of God written on their faces.

"What happened Bhavna?" Ramesh asked. He was now on the edge.

But Bhavna could not get herself to tell the truth because it seemed ludicrous. She shook her head to clear it. She could have sworn that she had seen a fire at her feet. But now everything was normal. Maybe it was just her imagination, she thought.

"A rat . . . a rat scurried across . . ." she made up the story as it came to her.

The unit members all burst out laughing as they realized that it was merely a rat that had scared their police inspector heroine.

"All right. Back to your positions. Going for take!" The Chief AD announced.

The shoot resumed. And again and again, Bhavna faltered. It was as if someone just erased her memory clean at that precise moment, robbing her of thought and speech.

"Sir, I can't explain it. Every time I go to say my dialogue . . ." she hesitated, "I keep forgetting . . . it's not forgetting but as if something is preventing me from saying the dialogues. Like my head is just wiped clean."

"Bhavna you are just psyching yourself. It is okay to forget dialogues," Ramesh tried to encourage her.

"I didn't forget!" Bhavna raised her voice out of sheer frustration. "Check for yourself . . ." saying this she rattled of the monologue without a hitch.

Ramesh chewed on his lower lip, unable to comprehend the eerie situation.

"Alright. Alright." He pacified Bhavna. "We will shift your location to the other room. Let's see if you find that comfortable."

"I am sorry!" Saying this Bhavna teared up.

"*Arre!* Bhavna, relax beta! It's okay. You will get through this scene. You go back to your vanity and rest. Let me speak to Shantanu." Saying this Ramesh went off to brief the DOP.

Bhavna lay down on the bed in her vanity van. She was staring at her own reflection in the mirror placed on the ceiling above the bed. She felt cold. She shivered as she thought of what she had just experienced. She could not find any logical explanation, except that she had gotten psyched by Santosh dada's story, and then what had happened to Smriti.

 *She closed her eyes. When she opened them, everything around her was dark. She sat up on the bed. There was no sound coming in from the outside. She swore

---

*   If you want to read along the following portion that's marked in bold with its own background music, then scan the QR Code to access the music and get ready to immerse yourself in the story.

that she had not fallen asleep but had just shut her eyes for a few seconds.

"Namit!" She screamed, while trying to find her mobile phone on the bed.

She heard a noise from the other room.

"Namit?" She asked, hoping that her assistant had come to help her.

She sniffed. *'Is someone burning dry leaves outside the vanity van?'* she thought to herself. And then, she suddenly realized what the smell was . . . it was the distinct smell of a burning *beedi*. It was strong. Namit did not smoke beedi . . . in fact Namit did not smoke at all! She began hyper-ventilating at the thought that there was a stranger in the other room . . .

"Kaun hai?" (Who's there?) Bhavna screamed feebly in the dark, afraid that someone would reply. She didn't want anyone to reply. She wanted it to be a manifestation of her imagination. There was silence. She heaved a sigh of relief.

"Bakwaas nahi hai!" (It's not nonsense) A male whisper floated to her from the other room.

The whites of her eyes glowed as her eyes widened in terror. She had clearly heard the voice. She wanted to scream for Namit, but her throat felt parched.

Someone moved the table in the other room. A laugh was heard.

The lights in the vanity van suddenly came back. Bhavna jumped with fright. She looked

around. She found her phone and quickly called Namit.

Namit rushed in.

"What happened?" he asked in a state of panic. Bhavna had sounded agitated and nervous over the call.

"Why was the vanity dark?" she screamed at him.

"The generator . . . the generator had some issue. But it was gone for just ten seconds or so!" Namit was taken aback at Bhavna's exaggerated reaction to such a small issue.

"There was somebody in the outside room, when it was dark . . ." she took a deep breath, "Can you smell it . . . can you get the smell of beedi? The man was smoking a beedi!"

Namit inhaled but could not discern any traces of beedi smoke.

"There's no smell of beedis!" Namit said and then added, "And no one entered your vanity van. I was standing just outside. Are you okay? Should I call a doctor?"

Bhavna just shook her head.

Namit's walkie crackled to life, making Bhavna jump.

"Namit. Please get Bhavna ma'am to set. I am outside her vanity."

"Tell makeup dada to do my touch up there." Saying this Bhavna exited the vanity van and accompanied by the AD walked toward the shooting area.

Even though she tried, she was unable to forget what had just happened. In her head she kept hearing the voice . . . and she could still get the acrid smell of the beedi.

"We have changed the location. Let's hope for the best," Ramesh patted Bhavna's back like a father encouraging his child.

As she walked into another part of the derelict mill, a *panditji* walked past her, while muttering some incantations and holding a *diya* in his hand.

"What is a panditji doing here?" She asked Santosh dada who was touching up her make up.

"After your experience in the adjoining room, Production Head called in a priest to bless the place. I think no one wants to take a chance. You are ready for the shot," Santosh dada tucked a loose strand of her hair behind her ear, gave her a final dekko and then walked out of the frame.

"Silence on the set. Going for take," the Chief AD yelled.

Bhavna quickly went over the lines in her head at a breakneck speed. She had always loved the stage. And every time, she had felt butterflies in her stomach just before her entry. She would stand in the wings going over her opening dialogue repeatedly, in her head . . . afraid that she would forget her lines. But every single time, when she set foot on the stage with trepidation in her heart, everything would sail smoothly as the first lines would be uttered by her. All the fear would dissipate. Her lines would come to her on cue like she had lived that moment a thousand times over. But today it had been different. It had felt weird. It had never happened before.

As she stood waiting nervously for the director to shout "Action," Bhavna's mind kept replaying the voice, the smell, the story . . .

Somewhere in the back of her mind she heard a distant, dull "Action." She took in a deep breath and started walking toward the camera.

She nailed it in one take. The crew burst into applause. Ramesh Dutt came and congratulated Bhavna, "That was awesome! This one is going to be a hit! I can feel it in my bones."

Suddenly a blood-curdling scream was heard from somewhere deep inside the cavernous crevices of the mill. Everybody turned around, their eyes wide with fear. It first appeared as an orange glow. It started running toward the crew with a scream. Bhavna stood transfixed, rooted at the spot. Her eyes unwavering; locked on to the strange vision unfolding before her.

The crew members were screaming and trying to run away, when somebody yelled, "Get water! It's Panditji!"

It was the priest who had been called to do a puja to ward off evil spirits. His kurta and dhoti were on fire. Some of the crew members doused him with water. Another crew member turned on the fire extinguisher on him. The priest collapsed on the ground.

An ambulance was called. Luckily, his face had not been burnt. His hands and legs had burn injuries.

"What happened?" Ramesh asked.

The priest was exhausted and was squirming in pain.

"I was doing a pooja—when suddenly the diya in my hand exploded into a ball of fire and before I could do anything, my clothes were ablaze! It was as if someone deliberately caused the fire to jump on to me." The priest took another sip of water.

Ramesh would have laughed, had it been on any other day. But today was different. There were series of things happening which belied human understanding. The ambulance arrived and the panditji was escorted to the hospital.

"Let's call for a dinner break," Ramesh announced. He had to think about what needed to be done. The bizarre incidents had spooked him and yet, on the other hand he had a film to complete. There were crores riding on the film. He was contemplating packing up from this location and finding a similar one to finish the shoot.

"Sir, to find a similar location will take us at least two to three days and then we have to see the availability. There is Vasai Fort, but for that we will need the permission from the Government, ASI (Archaeological Society of India). We are talking of at least five to seven days before we can shoot again," Pedro the Head of Production was sitting with Ramesh going over the possibilities.

Ramesh was stuck between a rock and a hard place.

*****

Bhavna searched for her phone charger. It wasn't to be found. Her phone battery was on its last legs. She remembered that she probably had left it in her car. She tried to call Namit, but his phone was switched off. She stepped out of her vanity van.

"Have you seen Namit, my assistant?" she asked one of the crew members.

"No, ma'am" the man replied and hurried toward the food tent.

She let out a sigh of irritation. She started walking toward the food tent. She knew her driver could be found there.

As soon as she entered, there was a murmur in the tent. The crew B members were not used to being in close proximity with the stars and here was the heroine of the film standing in their food tent!

Immediately, Nakul stood up from the crowd. She looked at him. He was holding a plate of food and was midway through his meal.

"Nakul, give me the car keys. I need to get something from the car," she reached out her hand for the keys.

Nakul immediately put his plate of food down on the table, "Ma'am I will get it for you. What do you need?"

"Nakul, please continue eating. It's okay. It's my mobile charger. I will get it. Please finish your meal properly," Bhavna instructed Nakul who handed her the car keys.

Bhavna still dressed in her cop uniform, walked toward the car park area. A few cars stood in the silence. The area was empty. Everyone was busy having their dinner. She scanned the lot for her car and spotted it. She walked toward it. The sound of crunching gravel accompanied her each step. She unlocked the car and got into the back seat. The smell of the leather and the car perfume soothed her nerves. She was back on familiar territory.

She looked around the seats for her charger. It wasn't there. She looked down on the floor of the car and spotted her mobile charger nestled in a corner of the floor mat. She smiled to herself and picked it up.

As soon as Bhavna sat back in her seat, she screamed! Just outside her car window was a man. Dishevelled, a face covered in soot and lesions. There were wisps of smoke floating up from him. Bhavna couldn't move. The man smiled at her. His eyes were dark pools of black ink. Bhavna's eyes widened in fear as the man puffed on a beedi. The last thing that Bhavna heard before she blacked out was the raspy voice of the man saying, *"Bakwaas nahi hai."*

****

Ramesh had decided to continue shooting at Mukesh Mills. He could not afford to delay the movie any further. He had discussed with Shantanu how best they could combine shots and try and knock off the climax as soon as possible.

Smriti was well enough to continue the shoot. She was brought in, and her close ups and dialogs were quickly filmed. And so the final face-off between the villain and the lady cop was left to be filmed. It was an elaborate fight sequence—the symbolic thrashing of evil by good.

"Are you ready for the shoot?" Namit asked Bhavna who was seated in front of the mirror, blankly staring into it. There was no reply from her. Bhavna got up mechanically and exited the van. Namit tried to make a conversation with her. But it seemed that Bhavna was lost in her own thoughts.

Bhavna quietly took her position, as instructed by Ramesh and Shantanu. Ramesh debriefed her about the scene. But there was no response from Bhavna. She just stood there with her head bowed low listening to Ramesh.

Ramesh thought of asking her if she was okay but decided against it. *Maybe she was just getting into the zone. Maybe she was just method acting*, he thought to himself. So he just let her be.

"Okay everybody. Silence on set. Going for take!" The Chief AD announced.

The camera came to life. The sound recordist gave a thumbs up. The clapper boy gave the 'clap' and exited the frame.

"And . . . Action!" Ramesh said over the PA system.

Bhavna was supposed to kick down a door and enter, but she just stood there. And before Ramesh could call a 'cut' Bhavna looked up and stared at him. Her eyes were bloodshot. Ramesh recoiled. Bhavna screamed. The scream rent through the air, making an HMI light burst into flames. The crew members screamed. And before Ramesh could react, Bhavna swiftly crossed over to Ramesh and held him by his collar.

This wasn't Bhavna anymore, Ramesh was staring into the face of a demon. Her skin had turned ashen. Her eyes were on fire. There were cracks in the foundation and make up making her look like broken porcelain doll that had been glued back together.

Bhavna let out a low growl and then screamed in a raspy man's voice, *"Yahan se chale jao, yeh hamari jagah hai, maine mana kiya tha naa mat aana, chale jao" Yahaan se chale jao! Yahaan se chale jao!"* (Go from here! This is our place! I had warned you not to come here! Go from here!)

The crew members screamed. The little children started crying. With one hand, Bhavna lifted Ramesh off the ground. His feet dangled in the air. He was like a rag doll in the hands of this monster. Bhavna flung Ramesh through the air. He landed a few meters away.

Bhavna stood there—her hair had come undone. She cocked her head to one side and stared at the circle of crew members standing around her.

And then she collapsed like an inflatable whose air had suddenly been sucked out. She lay there in a heap. No one dared to move. They could not believe what they had just witnessed.

Ramesh sat on the ground a few feet away from Bhavna, who now slowly got up and clutched her head in agony. She looked around at the crew members staring at her. She broke down and hugged herself.

The shoot was cancelled immediately. The story of the

shoot spread like wildfire across the film industry. It would be two weeks before Ramesh would be able to finally film the climax. Bhavna would go on a sabbatical for a year after the filming concluded.

Mukesh Mills continued to be used for filming, and as wedding venue till a few years ago. The ruins still stand, overlooking the waters of the Arabian Sea, waiting perhaps to be razed to the ground and a new commercial complex, or a posh housing society to emerge from its ruins.

****

DOW HILL
KURSEONG

Kurseong is located about 30 kilometers from Darjeeling. A quaint hill station which is known for its beautiful vistas, orchid gardens, forested hills and tea plantations. It also boasts of one of the most alleged haunted places of India—Dow Hill. A hill located above the town surrounded by pine forests and home to two renowned residential schools. The locals refer to the area as 'Death Road' where sightings of a headless ghost, the presence of a haunted school, and a boy's spirit that wanders around keep the stories alive.

THE
HEADLESS GHOST

Kurseong, 1978

The forest was bathed in the sounds of the cicadas. The moon was nowhere to be seen, hidden behind the dark clouds and the thick blanket of fog that enveloped the forest.

Sonam wiped his brow. The task of cutting wood even in the dead of winter, resulted in a bout of sweat. Upesh looked around and then egged on Sonam.

"*Chito gara.* (Work faster) The faster we finish the job, the quicker we get out of here. I don't want the Forest Officer to chase us again!"

"This is the last one. Come on!" Saying this Sonam got back at hacking the tree.

The rhythmic sound of their axes meeting wood echoed through the pine forest.

"It doesn't matter how many times I come here, but the forest always gives me the creeps!" Upesh muttered.

The forest he was referring to was between the Forest Department Office and Dow Hill. This stretch of road was referred to as *Mornay Baato* (Death Road). Stories of Dow Hill being haunted were passed from each generation to the next. Upesh and Sonam, two local woodcutters had grown up hearing the stories of a headless ghost that walks the forest. But they had to fill their stomachs and earn money. So here they were, in the dead of night, trying to get wood illegally. The Forest Department protected this forest that housed pine, acer timber, chestnut and oak trees.

Somewhere a jackal howled. The two wood cutters stopped their work to take a look. The jackal sounded near. But they could barely see anything through the fast-gathering fog.

"Let's get out of here before we get attacked by . . ." Sonam was cut short as Upesh admonished him.

"Hey! Don't take it's name! Come on let's go!"

They shoved the chopped wood into their bamboo *doko* and heaved it over their head. The strap pressed down on top of their heads, acting as a fulcrum to balance the weight and enable them to carry it on their backs. They started walking gingerly through the forest. Their feet squashing the dried leaves on the forest floor.

"Baato kahan xa?" (Where's the road?) Sonam stopped and looked around. The fog had made them lose their way.

"Let's just keep walking. At worst, we will at least come out near the Forest Office!" Upesh advised. They kept walking.

They had been chopping wood for the better part of an hour and that had kept them warm. But now, with no activity, the cold was slowly seeping into their bodies. As they spoke, their breath vaporized into puffs of smoke. They had deliberately not brought a torch, fearing that it would give them away to the forest officer.

Suddenly, they heard a low growl. It seemed to be only a few feet away. They halted in their tracks.

"I think it's the jackal," saying this Upesh pulled out his axe, which had been tucked at his waist, prepared to ward off any attack.

With each step they took, they kept looking around them in anticipation of the jackal leaping toward them from within the blanket of fog.

"Have you noticed the crickets have also stopped chirping?" Sonam whispered.

Upesh suddenly became aware of the impregnable silence that they were locked within. The forests of Kurseong always had the constant sound of the cicadas rubbing their wings. The sound was part of their life—the endless *tzzzzzzzzz!* So this silence was bizarre.

A rustle to their left made them aware of the impending danger. Sonam and Upesh both took the dokos off their head as they readied themselves to face the onslaught with the axes in their hands. Silence. And then a rustle from their right.

"How is the jackal traveling so fast from one side to the other?" Sonam was bewildered.

"Maybe it's not one, but two jackals . . . or perhaps more . . ." Upesh let the sentence hang in mid-air before it got absorbed by the fog.

A low growl. A rustle of leaves. And there, right in front of them, stood the silhouette of a headless man. The two friends shrieked and ran for their lives in different directions. Stumbling through the forest floor, Upesh fell, crawled, got up and ran again. He wanted to put a distance between what he had just seen and his precious life.

From childhood, he had heard stories about Dow Hill being haunted. It seemed everybody in Kurseong had a story or two that they had heard about *Mornay Baato*! Upesh screamed and ran as fast as he could. Upesh looked over his shoulder to see if the thing was pursuing him or not. There was nobody. The forest was silent again. Upesh could hear his own heart thumping. Wisps of vapor came out of his mouth with his rhythmic panting, making him look like a steam train ready to take off.

"Sonam?" Upesh whispered. When there was no response, he raised his voice by a few decibels, "Sonam?" He was met with silence. Upesh managed to find the road that went down to Kurseong town. He ran as fast as he could.

The next morning, he was shaken awake by his wife Sashi, "Do you know what has happened to your friend?" Upesh had rushed out of his house to find a gathering of people outside Sonam's house. He walked, pushing through the crowd. And then he saw Sonam.

Sonam had a wild look in his eyes. His clothes were torn. His hair was disheveled. And he just kept saying, "He is coming. He is coming for us all."

Sonam never recovered. As he grew older, the younger generation looked at him as a madman of the town, often referring to him as "*Laata* (madcap) Sonam."

Maybe the trauma kept playing inside Sonam's head every day and night. For Upesh, he always remembered what he had encountered that night in the forests of Dow Hill, till his last breath.

****

1985

Suraj Thapa, the caretaker of the boys' school carried the tin trunk out on the front drive, where a Premier Padmini Fiat was waiting. *'Arijit Sen Class V'* was written on the side of the trunk in white paint.

Suraj was 45 years old and was the second generation in his family to serve at the school. He lived on the campus and was in-charge of ensuring the workers in all the departments did their job on time and efficiently. When the school shut down for the three-month long winter break, Suraj stayed back to keep an eye on the school, and get the annual maintenance supervised.

There was always some roof that leaked, or a broken guttering that led to rain dripping on the side of the building leading to a green carpet of moss that stuck on the wall like velcro. There was furniture to be repaired, electricals to be inspected, and more.

Suraj was the invisible computer program that ran the systems. The school shut in December and reopened in

March. December was the month when Suraj could relax. But post the New Year, it was back to work and doing the annual maintenance.

Suraj was a single dad. His wife had died a couple of years ago, leaving behind their 12-year-old daughter Bithika, who was a spitting image of her mom, and who daily reminded Suraj how much he missed Neera, his wife.

Bithika studied at the adjoining girls' school, situated a kilometer away. She stayed with her father on campus at the boys' school in his quarter, making a daily trip to school and back. During the winter break, Bithika would help her father with his work.

Arijit turned to hug his friend Rupert. They were both in the same class.

"I am sorry Rupert that you will have to stay behind at school for the winter hols," Arijit and Rupert were thick friends. Both of them lived in Calcutta. One in Bhowanipore, the other in the Anglo-Indian part of Calcutta—Ripon Lane.

"I will be okay," Rupert said as he hugged Arijit.

"I will ask my father to send you a parcel for Christmas. I will buy the jujubes and the sticks of barley sugar from New Market and send you!"

"Thank you. Write to me," Rupert said. Arijit walked toward the waiting taxi, in which his uncle was seated. He had come to take Arijit home. Arijit would travel to Siliguri and then to Bagdogra to take a flight to Calcutta.

Arijit suddenly turned back and whispered into Rupert's ear, "Whatever you do . . . don't go into the forest alone!"

At the mention of the forest, Rupert swallowed hard, "I will not. You will write to me?"

Arijit ran off and got into the taxi. "I will," yelled Arijit from his side of the car as it sped off and exited the main gates of the school.

"I am sorry about your parents," Suraj said as he put his arm around Rupert.

At the mention of his parents, Rupert's eyes welled up. He quickly wiped it with the back of his school blazer, leaving the wool moist and clinging on to the tiny droplets like dew on grass.

Three months ago, Rupert's parents had met with a car accident. They had stepped out to get a treat for dinner. The Bengal Hotel on Ripon Street made a delectable dish that went by the name of *Pagla Bhuna* (Crazy Roast)—a meat dish that was roasted for more than an hour on a low flame, giving the dish a smoky flavor. It was a favorite amongst the Anglo-Indian community that lived in the area. And so Rupert's parents had managed to get one portion of the *Pagla Bhuna* and were headed back to Ripon Lane, when a speeding bike mowed them down. It wasn't the bike so much—but the taxi coming in from the opposite direction, whose wheels found the soft heads of the Mr. and Mrs. Sharpe.

The school authorities having received no monthly letters for three months from Rupert's parents decided to send their Calcutta staff member to find out more. Mr. Das was surprised to see new tenants in the Sharpe's house, who were the harbingers of the tragic news. Rupert had an alcoholic uncle who was not fit enough to take care of the ward. And so the school decided to keep back Rupert and care for him during the winter holidays; buying some more time to decide what to do with the orphan.

"Come on now. I need to start locking up the school," Suraj said as he took out a large bunch of keys from his coat pocket. The keys had little bits of paper cello taped on them—each key had the number of the classroom written on it.

Suraj went about ensuring the lights were off in each classroom, the windows locked, before closing it for the winter.

"I hate this part of my job. Every year, all the kids leave, and I am faced with silent, empty classrooms. I miss the noise," Suraj padlocked a classroom and started walking to the next one.

"I miss my class friends too when I leave . . . when I used to leave for the holidays," there was a tinge of sadness in Rupert's voice.

"I am sure you will go home next winter. There is bound to be some relative of yours," Suraj lovingly tousled Rupert's hair.

"I am all alone. There's no one," Rupert's eyes seem to well up again. He had hated boarding school when he had arrived three years ago. But as months went by, Rupert fell in love with the place. The school was beautiful, he made new friends, and he loved playing cricket and football. And now with all his friends gone, the loneliness crept in. After all, what was an empty school without his friends?

"You are not alone. I am here and so is Bithika. She is just two years older to you. She has lots of books and toys that you can read and play with. I am sure the holidays will get over in a jiffy, and your friends will be back in no time!" Suraj knew the pain of losing someone. When his wife had passed away suddenly, he had felt lost and helpless.

A check-up for lower abdominal pain had led to the discovery of a tumor in her stomach. Suraj had immediately actioned further tests. He did not want to lose any time. Unfortunately, the tumor was cancerous, and at an advanced

182

stage. He realized that life had dealt him a bad hand from the beginning. He had no time to begin with. It was a losing battle.

"Why don't you go play in the garden? You will get bored watching me lock up classrooms! Check your watch. It's 10.30 a.m. now. I will serve lunch at 12 noon in my quarter. Is that okay Rupert?" Suraj pulled the woolen cap over Rupert's ears, "Don't catch a cold, now."

Rupert nodded and ran off toward the garden. Suraj watched him go. He knew that this kid was having a rough time. It would either scar him for life, or Rupert would emerge as a fighter at the end of this war.

The sky was azure blue. The crisp sunshine warmed Rupert as he stepped out into the little garden. From out of his pocket he pulled out two dinky cars. He sat down on the mud and with the help of a stick started marking out and digging a road. He next hunted for two Y-shaped twigs. He placed the twigs on the ground and put small pebbles around them for support. Next he tied a small rock to one a long, straight twig and placed it across the two Y-shaped ones. He smiled to himself. He had managed to create a checkpost.

With his hand he drove one of the cars toward the checkpost, all the while making the sound of the engine with his mouth. Just before the car could reach the miniature checkpost it hit something buried in the ground and turned over. Rupert crept closer to the bump to investigate. He tried to dig with his nails, but the object was buried tight in the soil. So with a twig, he started digging. Little by little an old tinbox appeared. It was rusty in parts, but still had the original print on it. Rupert pulled the tin box out of the mud and looked at it.

It was a green square tin box. The cover had the picture of a milkmaid holding her head with one hand, and in the other she held a wooden pail of milk. She was flanked on both sides by a cow and a goat. There was a rooster and a few ducks . . . or was it geese? In the background was an English cottage. On the top left hand corner it read 'Parle Gluco Biscuits.' It was an old biscuit tin.

Rupert could not believe his luck. He had played in the area so many times and yet he hadn't found this treasure. He was excited. He shook the box. Something rattled inside. He smiled to himself. He was happy that there were no other kids to lay claim to this treasure; or worse senior kids who would bully him and snatch it away.

He tried to open the cover. It was stuck. He bit his lower lip as he put all this strength into his two hands and tried to wedge his fingernails under the edge of the cover to try and pull it up. And slowly, inch by inch, the cover opened.

There were so many things inside the box! An old black-and-white photograph of a boy, a few colored beads, some coins, and a couple of toy soldiers. He looked at the coins. One was a copper coin that said 1 naya paisa in Hindi. There were two silver coins of 5 naya paisa, and 2 naya paisa denominations. All the coins were dated 1958.

The beads were made of glass and strung together like a small necklace. He picked up the two toy soldiers. Both of them were holding a gun in the firing position. Rupert picked up the photograph. It showed a blonde-haired boy standing straight and looking back with a deadpan expression. The boy seemed to be the same age as him, Rupert thought to himself. Rupert looked closely. Yes! The boy was wearing the school uniform! This was a picture of an old boy from the school. Rupert turned the photo around. At the back, there was a scrawl in a kid's handwriting that read *Russell. October 1958.*

Suddenly Rupert heard a creak. He looked around and his eyes fell on the set of swings in the garden. As he kept looking, one of the swings began to move. At first Rupert thought that *it was due to wind . . . but there was no wind blowing . . . and if it was the wind—wouldn't both the swings move?*

The swing gathered momentum and began sweeping longer arcs as if there was somebody invisible sitting on it. Rupert's eyes grew wide in fear. Keeping his eyes locked on the swing he started gathering his dinky cars, and he leaped up to run. He banged into someone. Rupert yelled in fright.

"Ouch! Look where you are going!" a girl was standing in front of him, rubbing her arm.

"I am sorry," Rupert apologized.

"Hi, I am Bithika. Dad asked me to come and meet you."

All Rupert could reply was, "The swing . . . the swing . . ."

"What happened to the swing?" Bithika asked perplexed.

"It moved . . . on its own!" Saying this Rupert turned to show Bithika the swing—but both the swings were frozen. Rupert looked stunned.

"It was moving . . . just a few seconds ago! I promise!"

Bithika looked at the stationery set of swings, "But it's not moving now! It must have been due to wind."

"But only one was moving . . . if it was the wind, wouldn't both the swings move?" Rupert tried to convince her. He desperately wanted her to realize that he wasn't lying.

Bithika smiled and patronized him, "Alright. So it was moving. But it's not moving now. So forget about it! What is that on the ground? Is that your box?"

"I found this. It was buried here," Rupert picked up the box and handed it to Bithika, "It is from 1958."

Bithika's eyes widened in amazement, "Wow! A real

treasure!" She went through the contents and stopped at the photograph.

"See his school uniform is the same as mine. And see his name is Russell and this is from 1958. Look at the back," Rupert was excited trying to show off his find.

Bithika turned the photograph around and examined it, "It looks like he was a student here. He must have buried it and forgotten about it. Lucky you!"

Rupert closed the box and held it close to his chest, lest the box decided to vanish on him. "Come, my father sent me to call you for lunch."

The two of them walked off. Rupert looked over his shoulder one last time, to take a look at the swing. It wasn't moving. *I must have imagined it*, he thought to himself.

Suraj lived on the ground floor of the old Victorian building. His home comprised a sitting room, kitchen, a bathroom, and a large bedroom. Rupert had never been here, and so stopped to look around the living room when he entered.

"Lunch will be served in ten minutes," Suraj's voice floated out from the kitchen. There was a framed photograph on the mantle above the fireplace that caught Rupert's eye. It had a beautiful lady dressed in a sari, smiling at the camera.

"Who's this?" Rupert asked Bithika.

Bithika shuffled her feet, "That's my mom."

"She is very pretty," Rupert remarked.

"She was . . . she died," Bithika was succinct.

"I am sorry," Rupert looked at Bithika, "My mother is dead too. And my father."

The two children looked at each other. They instantly knew that they were bound by their tragic circumstances.

"I am sorry. I didn't knew," Bithika said.

"You mean . . . I didn't know! That's the correct way," Suraj entered with a tray of food. Looking at the kids, he suddenly realized that he might have just walked in on something serious.

"What happened? Why the long faces?"

"Nothing," both the kids said in unison, and they were startled at their synchronized answer, and immediately looked at each other and smiled.

As they ate lunch, Suraj spoke up, "Bithika, you need to teach Rupert math. Father Sherwood requested that Rupert should not fall behind in his lessons."

"So what did you do this morning?" Suraj asked Rupert who was busy stuffing his mouth with home-made food, which was a far cry from the food that they got at the school's mess.

"I found a box of treasure. I dug it from under the ground," Rupert spoke with his mouth full. He looked comical trying to keep the contents of his mouth from falling out while speaking.

"Not with your mouth full. That's disgusting!" Bithika teased.

"Listen both of you. Whatever you do, please do not head out into the forest, especially Death Road," Suraj did not want to be an alarmist, but he knew that he had to forewarn the kids from loitering to places that were out of bounds.

Rupert looked up immediately, "That's what Arijit told me before he left."

"And rightfully so. It gets fogged over and you cannot see your hands even if they are an inch from your face," Suraj added.

"But why is it called Death Road?" Bithika had heard the name many times but did not have a clue how the place had earned its name.

"I don't think you kids need to know," Suraj avoided the topic, but Bithika was insistent, "Come on papa you have to tell us."

"You will get scared. Both of you are too young to hear such stories! Maybe in two or three years' time."

"We won't get scared," Bithika piped up. Rupert was in two minds, especially after the incident with the swings. One part of his mind was curious to find out, while the other part screamed inside his head and urged him to close his ears.

"Alright. Our school is surrounded by a forest that is over 200, or perhaps, 300-years-old. It is said that in the forest, there live many mysterious spirits and magical creatures. Some bad, some good. But one of the spirits has been scaring and tormenting people for many years.

Just as he ended the sentence, a piercing whistle rang out which startled the kids who jumped up and screamed.

Suraj laughed, "I thought you said you weren't going to get scared! You are scared of a pressure cooker!" The kids looked embarrassed.

"We are not scared. It just . . . it just made us jump, that's all." Bithika tried to put up a brave front.

"So should I stop or continue?"

"Please continue papa!"

Suraj cleared his throat and prepped himself as he knew he was coming to the scary part of the story.

"So this one spirit that has been tormenting people . . ." He paused for a few seconds and then continued, "It has no head."

"A headless ghost?" Rupert almost whispered it to himself.

"Mr. Douglas Byrne was an Irishman who lived near the school. At that time there was no school of course. This must have been early 1850s. He was a landowner and was quite a ruthless man. He tortured the local people, forced them to work for low wages, and was a much-despised man. The story goes that Mr. Douglas had a local servant boy Binod whose job was to follow him like a shadow and tend to his needs. This boy who was 25-years-old at that time, fell in love with Mr. Douglas' daughter who was 17. When Mr. Douglas found out, he was enraged and punished the boy with whip-lashes. And when that did not seem enough, he ordered the beheading of the boy. Since that time, it is this boy's headless ghost that roams around the forest and many locals mention that the ghost has beheaded other people as revenge. That is how the road near the forest earned its name *Mornay Baato*.

Rupert and Bithika had their mouths open, their slack jaws were indicative of how stunned they were on hearing the origin story.

"Have you ever seen him?" Rupert asked in a barely audible voice.

"The headless ghost? Hahaha!" Suraj laughed, "No. I don't believe in this story at all. Yes, Mr. Douglas may have beheaded someone in rage, but its ghost roaming around the forest seems too far-fetched."

Rupert could not get the image of the phantom swings out of his head, "Is our school haunted?"

Suraj looked at Rupert and smiled, "That is enough ghost stories for one day. Just don't go into the forest. Forget the headless ghost, I am more scared of you two getting lost!"

Rupert spent the rest of the afternoon and evening watching television in Bithika's house. In Kurseong, it was easier to catch the television signals from Bangaldesh, than India's Doordarshan. With an outdoor antenna and a television signal booster, people of the hills of West Bengal were privy to classic American television shows that aired on Bangaldesh TV. 5.00 p.m. was cartoon time everyday. And 7.00 p.m. was time for series like *Remington Steele, The A-Team, Knight Rider* and more. The school usually hosted a movie screening every month, but to be watching cartoons on television was a treat for Rupert.

There was a small dorm adjoining Suraj's quarters. And as per the instructions left by Father Sherwood, Rupert was to sleep in the small dorm.

"Papa can I sleep in the dorm too with Rupert?" Bithika was hopeful that she be allowed by her father, who of course turned her down, "It's not allowed. Even a boys' school closed for the holidays remains a boys' school. You can be together again in the morning. And anyway, he is just next door."

When Father Sherwood had told him about the boy, Suraj had offered his quarter for the boy to sleep in at night.

"Father, I can shift one of the beds into my sitting room. The boy can sleep there."

"Suraj, we are a school and we have to abide by the rules. The boy will have to sleep in the dorm. No mingling with staff members. He has to grow up and be a man," Father Sherwood was a strict Englishman who always did everything by the book. He had run the Boys' school like clockwork with not one shoelace out of place. He had been working at the boys' school since the 1950s. During the winter holidays, Father Sherwood would travel to local parishes and even to other parts of the country to oversee projects and spread the word of God. He was currently in Siliguri looking at the construction of a new church.

And so Suraj had no other option but to fix Rupert's bed in the small dorm, which was usually reserved for the new admissions that came in every year.

Suraj walked to the dorm holding Rupert's hand in his.

The tiny dormitory had four beds on either side of the room, placed against the walls in a row.

Rupert's dorm was a much larger one and he had been apprehensive that he would have to sleep in the dorm alone. But the sight of this smaller dorm gave him a sense of relief.

Suraj had already prepared one of the beds. The other seven beds had folded mattresses on them.

"Rupert, don't forget to say your prayers. Good night. We will see you in the morning. And keep this torch with you, in case the electricity goes off." Saying this Suraj handed him a small torch.

"Good night, sir." Saying this Rupert knelt at the side of his bed and said the Lord's Prayer aloud . . .

"Our Father, who art in heaven
Hallowed be thy name . . . "

When he finished, he went and switched off the light. Immediately the dorm was plunged into darkness. The beds were now bathed in the clear blue moonlight that was beaming in from the large arched windows. Rupert quickly ran to his bed, and dived in, pulling the quilt and blanket over his head. The bed was cold in spite of the blanket and the quilt covering it. The pillow felt like a block of ice on his cheeks as he put his head on it. He pulled his woolen cap as much as he could to cover his cheeks.

He could hear himself breathing under the covers. Rupert peeped out from under the covers with one eye. His eye scanned the empty dormitory. The story about the beheading and the headless ghost had spooked Rupert. But he had wanted to appear brave in front of Bithika, and therefore had continued listening to the story.

From the corner of his eye Rupert saw something move outside one of the windows. He could not make out what it was. It had appeared as a black shape that had darted across the window. *Was it a wild animal from the forest?* Rupert thought to himself. He had heard senior boys talking about wild animals visiting the school when it is shut for the winter holidays.

Suddenly from the darkness between the two beams of moonlight, a figure appeared. It stood at the centre of the dormitory. Rupert's throat went dry as he realized that it is the same boy whose photo he had found earlier. The small boy was wearing the same school uniform. His face was bloodied.

"Russell!" Rupert repeated the name in his mind having recognized him from the photo.

Rupert could not look away. He was frozen. The boy slowly lifted his right arm and held it out toward Rupert.

"Rupert" The boy said Rupert's name with a slow drawl, "Give my stuff back!"

Rupert found the courage to make his move. He dived back under the covers and switched on the torch that had been given to him by Suraj sir. Rupert was hyper-ventilating. His ears were on alert trying to hear what was going on beyond his flimsy tent of protection.

He could not hear anything. There was silence. Just then a force pulled the bed covers and the quilt, which was protecting him, leaving Rupert sitting on the bed too scared to move. His scream had been stifled in his throat. Rupert had expected Russell to be standing at the foot of his bed, but there was nobody in the dormitory. He shone the beam from his torch around him. There was nobody.

The beam now traveled across each bed. There were only upturned mattresses. The beam now lit up the last bed in the dark corner of the room, untouched by the moonlight. There is nobody there. Rupert heaved a sigh of relief.

Rupert knew that the only way he could be safe was to go and seek Suraj sir's help. Rupert gingerly got off the bed and started tip-toeing toward the wall with the electrical switches. He wanted to switch on the lights of the dorm. His childlike head had figured out that ghosts cannot play hide and seek if it is not dark.

The old, wooden floor-boards creaked under the shifting weight as Rupert walked across them. Each step was accompanied by a groan, like an old house waking up from a long slumber.

Suddenly a hand popped out from under one of the beds and brushed against his ankle. Rupert stumbled and ran to the light switch and flicked it on. The dormitory was immediately bathed in the yellow hue from the interspersed naked bulbs hanging from the ceiling. Rupert was panting. He looked around the dorm. Everything seemed normal. He looked toward his bed and his bed covers and quilt were placed on the bed! *But how can that be? They were pulled off from the bed . . . they were on the floor when he last checked! Had he just imagined all of it?*

Rupert looked at a hand popping out from under the bed. His eyes widened in fear for a moment before he realized it was the stuffed hand of a doll. Rupert slowly walked to the bed and pulled the doll from under it. It was a stuffed joker.

Maybe he had imagined everything . . .

Rupert let the lights of the dorm remain switched on, as he crept back into bed. He didn't want to bother Suraj sir as everything seemed normal. He immediately fell into a deep sleep, unaware that Russell was seated on the opposite bed watching him.

"It's okay Rupert. It's nothing to be embarrassed about. I used to do it when I was a kid," Suraj said as he pulled the mattress off the bed. Rupert had wet his bed.

Rupert stood there with his head lowered. He had never wet his bed before this. He had seen other smaller children in the dorm being teased and taunted when they had done it. And he had joined the gang as well to make fun of these small children. And here he was, his night suit soaked in his own piss.

"I have heated water for you. Have a bath and put on fresh clothes. I will clean up," Suraj pulled the covers and the sheets too, bundling them up for a wash. Usually, this was done by the Dorm wardens and their assistants. But Suraj had to do everything as the staff was on leave for the winter.

Rupert emerged out of the bathroom at Suraj's quarter. He wiped his head with the pink towel which had his name written on it with marking ink. He looked at the writing and remembered his mother who had 'marked' all his clothes before he had left for school.

"You are such a big boy and you did *susu* in the bed?" Bithika asked and stifled a laugh.

Rupert glared at her.

"Alright. I will not tease you! Sorry!" Bithika said as she held her ears in mock apology.

"There was somebody in the dorm last night," Rupert whispered.

"How is that possible? We three are the only ones at school."

"It was the same boy from the photograph! Russell from 1958."

Bithika did not know whether to laugh or believe Rupert, "You mean from the treasure box? But that kid is probably old or even . . . dead by now!"

"I swear I saw him. It was Russell's ghost. He called out my name and he wanted his treasure box back!" Rupert fought back tears as he felt frustrated seeing Bithika not believing him, again. He grabbed Bithika's hand, "Come I will show you!"

Rupert took Bithika to the adjoining mini dormitory.

"I was here in my bed. And he stood where you are standing now," Rupert explained.

"It was dark. And you might have imagined it all, after hearing Papa's story?" Bithika threw a possibility out into the wind.

"No. it wasn't fully dark. I saw him in the moonlight. His face had blood on it. He said he wanted me to give him back his stuff!" Rupert rattled off, hoping that Bitika would somehow get convinced.

"Do you want to tell Papa?" she asked.

"No. He will not believe me, just like you don't." Rupert's lips quivered and he clenched his jaw.

"I don't know Rupert whether I believe it or not. It just sounds strange and unbelievable. Anyway, I need to teach you math. Come on, let's go," saying this Bithika held out her hand. Rupert did not take it. Bithika raised her eyebrows in an expression that summed up 'whatever.'

Suraj tidied up the table after they had had dinner. He addressed Rupert.

"I shouldn't have told you both the ghost story yesterday. It's probably because of that you got scared and you did . . ." Suraj did not finish the sentence and Rupert felt embarrassed in front of Bithika.

"You keep this bell with you." Saying this Suraj handed a windup mechanical bell, the kind used on office desks, to Rupert.

"If you get scared, press the bell. I will be able to hear it. Now off to bed. Tomorrow both of you can go into town for ice cream."

Bithika and Rupert beamed in delight.

Suraj escorted Rupert back to the dorm. "I have made a fresh bed for you. Don't forget to say your prayers. And keep the light on. There's no need to shut it."

Saying this Suraj went back to his quarter.

Rupert quickly took a look around the dimly lit dorm, and then dived straight into bed, pulling the covers over his head. Under the tent, he turned on his torch. He waited for a few minutes, and then gathering courage he peeped out from under the covers. Everything seemed normal.

He slowly bent over, overhanging from the side and shone the torch under his bed. The coast was clear. He got up, relieved. He knelt on the bed and said his prayers. He kept the bell on top of the coop beside his bed. From inside the coop he took out an Indrajal Comic and began reading.

Rupert fell asleep within minutes. The dim, yellow lights in the dormitory flickered for a few seconds. And then, it was pitch darkness. There was no moon in the sky to illuminate the dorm.

One of the beds creaked in the dark, followed by a boy's giggle.

Rupert stirred in his sleep.

The floorboards creaked in the darkness as somebody walked about in the dormitory. Rupert's eyes flew open.

It took him a ten seconds to realize that the lights in

the dorm were out. He looked around the dorm. His heart thumped in inside his chest.

*A laugh from within the darkness.

Rupert slowly turned on his torch and with his shaking hands scanned the room with the beam of light.

Suddenly from within a dark patch in the room—a hand swiftly appeared holding a wooden rattle. The rattle rotated making a horrible loud noise. Rupert watched in shock and horror. And just as suddenly it had appeared, the hand slid back into darkness. And there was silence again.

Rupert quickly looked for the bell which he had kept on top of the coop. It wasn't there. He started hyper-ventilating. *I put it here . . . maybe it fell on the ground . . .*

Rupert shone the beam of light on the floor—the bell was nowhere to be seen.

With the wooden rattle rotating in one hand, Russell's ghost slid out from the darkness. His face was bloodied. His blonde hair was matted with blood. He walked slowly toward Rupert. The sound of the rattle and the creaking floorboards created an eerie background score.

"Looking for this?" Russell smiled as he held out the bell in the other hand.

---

*   If you want to read along the following portion that's marked in bold with its own background music, then scan the QR Code to access the music and get ready to immerse yourself in the story.

Rupert was frozen. It was as if something was holding him down.

Russell stood at the end of Rupert's bed and whispered, "He will come for you and do what he did to me."

Suddenly a trickle of blood appeared at Russell's throat. Russell tried to speak. But more blood flowed out from his mouth. And it was as if Russell was struggling to breathe. The blood began frothing and foaming in his mouth forming air bubbles that slid down the side of his chin.

Rupert screamed. But no one could hear him. *If it's my imagination it will go away*, he thought. And then he closed his eyes to shut out what he was seeing.

When he opened his eyes, he recoiled in fear. His bed was in the middle of the forest. It was cold, and the fog was rolling in.

How did I get here? What is going on? Rupert panicked as he felt his bladder give up on him.

And out of the fog emerged a silhouette with a low growl. Rupert wanted to run. But he could not get out of the bed. He screamed, "Help me!" His voice echoed through the forest.

The silhouette walked toward him, and that is when Rupert noticed the figure had no head. Tears streamed down Rupert's face. The silhouette was holding an axe.

Rupert heard his name. His eyes flew open.

There was Suraj sir and Bithika standing beside his bed.

"What happened Rupert? You were screaming in your sleep!" Suraj sat down on Rupert's bed and immediately stood up. The bed was wet.

It took Rupert a few seconds before he realized that he was out of harm's way. There was bright sunlight streaming through the arched windows of the dormitory.

"I saw the ghost of the boy again . . . and then I was in the forest . . . and I saw the headless ghost! He was coming for me!" Saying this Rupert broke down.

Suraj shook his head in regret, "It is all my fault. I should not have told you both the story! And what was it again that scared you last night?" Suraj was cursing himself for assuming that the kids would brush his story aside. But obviously, Rupert hadn't.

"My bed was there in the forest, and he was coming to cut off my head!" Rupert repeated through his tears.

"If your bed was in the forest—then how come you are back here—and the bed is here? Rupert, it was all a bad dream," Bithika held Rupert around his shoulders.

"Alright. Rupert go for your shower and let me clean up your bed. Then after breakfast, both of you go to town. Have a fun outing. It will get all this off your minds."

****

Bithika and Rupert were excited. Walking downhill, they headed toward Kurseong town, which was approximately three kilometers away. The road from Dow Hill would take them right down to Kurseong train station.

The day was bright and warm. Rupert and Bithika kept walking without speaking with each other. Rupert could not fathom what had happened to him last night. And Bithika was now too scared to ask.

"Let's take the shortcut—we will be able to reach faster," saying this Bithika walked down a dirt track that ran into the forest.

"We aren't supposed to go in the forest," Rupert remembered both Suraj and Arijit's words of heed. But Bithika walked on, "Nothing will happen. And it's daytime!"

Rupert gulped. Bithika was way ahead of him. He did not want to be left behind and so ran to catch up with her.

"So what did you see exactly?" Bithika asked. But when she did not get any response from Rupert, she looked behind her. Rupert was rooted to a spot, about thirty feet behind her.

"What happened Rupert?" she asked as she hurried back to where he was standing and staring at something.

Bithika stood beside Rupert and followed his gaze. Her eyes widened.

There in front of them was a fork in the road, and a wooden marker that pointed to the fork. On the marker in red paint was written—*Mornay Baato*.

They both stood there transfixed in horror watching the dirt track go deep into the forest. The foliage on both sides of the dirt track created a tunnel or a canopy across the track. Rupert looked closely. It was as if the forest was breathing, and the tunnel was slowly inching toward them like an open hungry mouth, ready to swallow them up.

"Let's go from here," Rupert pleaded.

"Yes. I think that's a good idea!" Bithika said as they held each other's hands and ran down toward town.

A distant growl echoed through the forest. A gust of wind traveled across the forest floor, lifting up the dry leaves and making them whirl around in a macabre dance. The wind grew in intensity and it hit the wooden marker at the fork on the road.

The marker creaked and slowly turned. *'Mornay Baato'* was now pointed at the same road that the kids had taken from school. It seemed the spirits were laying out a trap.

****

Bithika and Rupert walked to the Kurseong train station. There was a train engine parked there. Rupert went up close to take a look at it. It was a beautiful, old engine. The driver who was up in the engine room blew the whistle which startled Rupert. The driver peeped out and waved. They both had a good laugh. The kids next headed to the bazaar area. There they encountered a *'boxy-walla'* whose name was derived from the huge tin box he carried over his head filled with savories like patties and puffs. Suraj had given money to Bithika and so she bought two chicken patties. Next, they headed to the ice cream shop where they bought two orange lollies. They sat on a bench and devoured the treat. The orange lolly melted and dribbled down their arms. And the kids slurped up the dribble as well. After all, ice cream could never be wasted. They loitered around town for a bit, heading into a small café opposite the railway station to have their lunch of masala *dosa*. The day was turning out to be quite a treat for the kids.

It was time now to head back up the road to school. The warm sun was slowly receding and there was a dip in the temperature. They started hurrying and walking. It had taken them 25 minutes to come downhill. But it would take them an hour at least to walk up. And they wanted to reach the safety of the school before it got dark.

They halted and took rest in between. The joy of a well-spent day was slowly fading like the sunlight as the duo walked back into their real world. And Rupert particularly did not like this real world after what he had endured for the past two nights.

Bithika and Rupert took the short-cut again, hoping to cut down on their walking time. The forest was quiet, except for the screeching of birds now and then and the slow dull background noise of the cicadas. They arrived at the fork in the road with the marker post.

Little did they know that the spirits were up to mischief.

Bithika stood below the marker and hesitated for a moment. Something seemed off—but she could not put her finger on it.

"Let's go. We are getting late," Rupert said, and without a thought, the duo entered the Death Road unknowingly.

They kept walking. Rupert caught hold of Bithika's hand. As they walked, they noticed that there were red ribbons and strings hanging from some of the trees. The ribbons were all eerily still. That is when it hit them.

"This is not the road we took when we were headed to town!" Bithika looked around her.

"We didn't pass these flags . . ." Rupert started and then the realization dawned upon them. The blood drained from their face, "This is not the road to school—we are on Death Road!"

They both looked at each other.

"Let's turn around and find our way back to the fork in the road," Bithika said as she grabbed Rupert's hand. But when they turned around they could not find the road behind them. As if the forest had come to life and covered the tracks . . . as if the foliage had surrounded them. They ran around in circles but could not find the dirt track. And then a sound alerted them. They both turned around.

The rustling of leaves—like someone was walking on them.

The sun was gone. And the forest seemed darker now. And the darkness was magnified by the foliage that cut off the daylight. The fog started crawling in silently, brushing against the trees as it headed for the kids. That is when they heard a low growl somewhere near . . . too close for comfort. The kids ran for their lives to beat both the fog and whatever had made that noise.

In the ensuing chaos, Bithika realized that Rupert was no longer with her! And Rupert realized that he was there all alone.

"Rupert!" Bithika screamed.

"Bithika!" Rupert was petrified. He was revisiting his terrifying dream again!

Bithika heard Rupert's voice through the thick fog!

"I can hear you! Where are you? Come toward my voice!" Bithika screamed.

Rupert heard Bithika's voice but could not find his way out of the thick wall of fog that had wrapped itself around him. Rupert ran blindly through the fog screaming Bithika's name. But no one replied. And then he stumbled and fell onto the forest floor.

His forehead hit the ground and Rupert winced in pain. He could feel something warm trickle down the side of his face.

He knew that it was blood. And then he heard the low growl from his dream. And out of the fog emerged the headless silhouette holding an axe.

Rupert screamed, "No! Please don't hurt me!" Rupert crawled on his fours to try and get away. The blood from his forehead tickled down to his eye, blurring his vision. He kept crying and pleading. The headless silhouette slowly followed him.

Rupert looked back and noticed spurts of blood exiting the stump on which the head had once rested. Rupert vomited. The dosa and the ice cream all regurgitated into a mush that now dribbled down Rupert's chin. He felt his bowels surrender, as he shat in his pants. He got up and stumbled and ran, with shit trickling down the insides of his legs.

And then he blacked out.

When he opened his eyes, Rupert was startled, before he realized that it was Suraj sir and Bithika looking at him. He was back in Suraj sir's quarter.

"Thank God you are okay," Suraj sighed in relief.

"What happened?" Rupert asked haltingly as if he was getting used to his voice for the first time.

"When I could not find you, I just ran. Thankfully I found the fork in the road and ran up to the school and got Papa. When we came back, we saw you lying unconscious at the fork on the road. And Papa carried you back and cleaned you up. The doctor is on his way."

"The marker was pointing the wrong way. And both of you took the Death Road. What happened out there?" Suraj asked.

"The headless ghost. I saw him. This time it wasn't a dream. He was there!" As he recalled, Rupert felt the fear creeping back into him.

Just then a knock was heard on the door. Suraj went and opened it. It was Dr. Rao. He was the visiting doctor for the school. He came in every Tuesday and Saturday to do a thorough checkup on the children when the school was in session.

Dr. Rao was a small man who walked with a slight hunch due to his advancing age. He had once served in the Armed Forces as a doctor. He was called 'teddy bear' lovingly by the students due to his cuddly face and kind eyes.

"Let me take a look," he said as he unboxed his large leather bag and extricated a stethoscope, and put it on Rupert's chest, "Okay now breathe in and out."

He then checked his temperature and blood pressure.

"Hmm. So Suraj sir has told me about what happened. You need to get rest. Nothing is wrong with you. Just get sleep and let your mind rest. In case you have a temperature, I am giving some medicines for you." Saying this Dr. Rao handed over some medicines from his cavernous bag to Suraj, before exiting.

Suraj turned to Rupert, "This ghost that you said you saw in the dorm, what did he look like?"

"I have a photo of him!" Rupert said.

Suraj looked dumbfounded, "What do you mean? How can you have a photo of a ghost?"

"Bithika, can you please get the box from my bedside coop?"

Bithika ran off to retrieve the treasure biscuit box.

"This is what I found three days ago when I was digging in the mud," Rupert said as Bithika handed the box to his father. Suraj opened the box, took the coins and the beads and then picked up the black and white photograph of the blonde-haired boy. He turned the photo around and gasped.

The two kids looked at him, wondering what was wrong.

"This boy . . . this . . . Russell," Suraj stammered and then composed himself.

"You know this boy?" Bithika asked, wondering how on earth did her father know an old boy from before his time in school.

"Yes. My father told me the story about Russell. Remember Mr. Douglas Byrne, the angry Irishman and Binod, the servant who fell in love with Byrne's daughter? It is supposedly Binod's headless ghost who is said to be roaming the forest. I did not believe the story till today. I did not know anyone personally who could vouch for a sighting. But today you did."

"You believe me?" Rupert asked, relieved.

"Yes, I do. And with this photo you have connected the dots," Suraj looked worried.

"What dots?" Bithika was inquisitive.

"I have called Father Sherwood. He should be here anytime now. He is the best person to tell you the story. I just know it from hearsay."

After rescuing Rupert, Suraj had called up Father Sherwood in Siliguri and had informed him. This was too big an event to not inform the boss about. Father Sherwood who was in Siliguri immediately said that he would head back to the school. The journey from Siliguri to Kurseong was an hour's drive.

Just at that moment, a knock was heard on the door. They all got startled.

Suraj, a fully grown man, was suddenly not taking any chances and so without opening the door he asked, "Who is it?"

"Father Sherwood here." The voice from beyond the door replied.

Suraj and the kids were relieved to hear a familiar voice. Suraj opened the door of his quarters to let Father Sherwood in.

The 65-year-old Father Sherwood went straight to Rupert and quickly knelt beside his bed and closed his eyes in prayer. He then arose, took out some Holy Water which he sprinkled on Rupert and the other two in the room. He kissed the gold crucifix on his neck and touched it to Rupert's forehead. And then he sat down.

"I believe you have got yourself caught in quite a mess!," Father Sherwood began.

Suraj handed the black and white photograph to Father Sherwood who took a look at it, flipping it from front to back.

"Russell Ainsworth, a fine lad he was," he said it almost to himself.

"You knew him?" Bithika asked.

"Of course I did. I joined the school in the 1957. I was just starting off," Father Sherwood nodded, like he was coming to terms himself with what he was about to narrate.

"I was a young man then. Father Lynn was in charge of the school. We were brought here fresh off the boat from Calcutta. I met Russell in 1957 the same year that I joined this school. His father was in charge of one of the tea gardens in Kurseong. So he studied here."

Father Sherwood picked up one of the toy soldiers from the biscuit tin and smiled.

"I remember Russell playing with these, like it was yesterday. He spent a lot of time out in the garden by himself creating imaginary worlds," Father Sherwood looked up at Rupert and reminisced, "So it's not a coincidence that you would be the one who found his hidden box. You are both alike in so many ways. And this box has been hidden for 27 years and no one found it. It took the imagination of a Rupert to unearth the treasures of Russell."

Suraj brought in tea for Father and himself and hot milk for the children. Father Sherwood continued.

"It was October 1958. Russell Ainsworth along with his three friends Richard Lucas, Randolph Richardson, and Tshering Tobgay had gone into the forest even though they knew it was forbidden. They got lost. When the children were reported missing at dinner time, Father Lynn organized a search party. I was amongst the 30 people who went into the forest that night." Father Sherwood paused. Revisiting the past had unearthed the tragic memories that he had buried like the treasure box. Rupert had managed to unearth that as well. He exhaled deeply before he resumed.

"We first found the three boys Richard, Randolph, and Tshering. They were lying unconscious on the forest floor. They had deep wounds on their hands and legs. But Russell Ainsworth was nowhere to be seen. When the boys came to consciousness, all they remembered was getting lost in the fog and then being attacked by something or a wild animal. We lit fire torches and ventured deeper into the forest and finally, we found Russell. He had been killed."

"Richard showed me his wound . . . on his neck . . . he said that the headless ghost had done it."

Rupert's voice was shaky. He was coming to terms with the fact that it had not been his imagination after all. It was Russell's ghost that he had met in the dorm.

Father Sherwood looked at the photo in his hand, "A police investigation was launched but no one was caught or accused of the crime. The locals believed that Russell was a victim of Binod, the headless ghost."

There was deathly silence in the room.

"Rupert," Father Sherwood took Rupert's hands in his. Rupert noticed that there were two missing fingers on his right hand. "I believe every word you have said, and everything you have seen. Over the years we had heard about Russell's ghost roaming around the school, but we had denied it, lest the kids get scared. And Russell was a harmless child. But I guess once you unearthed his beloved treasure box, he wanted it for himself. I am going to be keeping this," Saying this Father Sherwood got up to leave.

"Suraj, let Rupert sleep here in your quarter for tonight. I will be on campus tonight. Tomorrow I will need to do some work. Rupert, get some rest."

Saying this Father Sherwood left the place.

****

Father Sherwood walked into his bedroom where an old wooden cupboard was standing. He took out a key from his pocket and unlocked the cupboard. It was stacked with papers, artefacts, and religious items. He pulled out an old leather box. It was weathered and the leather was damaged in parts. He set it down on a table and opened it. On top of the box in faded gold calligraphy was the name 'Father Samuel Lynn.'

The box was lined in red satin. There was an old Bible bound in leather and gilded lettering. Beside it was a wooden cross. And there was a small decorative glass bottle that contained Holy water.

Father Sherwood opened the Bible, turned to the Book of Ephesians, and thumbed his way down to Chapter 6 verse 10 and started reading aloud,

"Finally, be strong in the Lord and in the strength of his might. Put on the whole armor of God, that you may be able to stand against the schemes of the devil. For we do not wrestle against flesh and blood, but against the rulers, against the authorities, against the cosmic powers over this present darkness, against the spiritual forces of evil in the heavenly places. Therefore take up the whole armor of God, that you may be able to withstand in the evil day, and having done all, to stand firm. Stand therefore, having fastened on the belt of truth, and having put on the breastplate of righteousness . . ."

The tin box kept in the next room began to rattle . . . Father Sherwood knew that Russell was listening, and he wasn't happy.

****

That night Suraj made Bithika and Rupert sleep in the bedroom. He did not want Rupert to be by himself.

"Thank you, sir," Rupert said as Suraj tucked the two children into bed, "Thank you for saving me today."

Suraj smiled, "You don't need to be scared tonight. We are all with you. The only thing you need to be scared about is Bithika's snoring!" He burst out laughing.

"Papa! That's so mean!" Bithika protested, "I don't snore!"

Rupert laughed. He felt safe.

****

It was past midnight. Father Sherwood sat in his study. His eyes locked on the tin box kept on the table. He wanted to see if Russell would come for it.

He must have dozed off when he heard the sound of a wooden rattle. Father Sherwood sprang up. There was silence in the room. *Had I heard the sound in my dreams?* he thought to himself.

He drew out the old wooden cross and held it up in front of him. As he watched, the tin box moved and slid on the table.

"Russell, if you are here. Go away." Father Sherwood said softly. The box stopped moving. Father Sherwood was sweating even though it was winter. He held out the cross in front of him—slowly moving it from side to side—trying to protect himself from the invisible demon.

The sound of the rattle echoed in the silence.

Rat-a-tat-a-tat-a-tat!

And Russell slowly appeared and stood behind Father Sherwood and giggled. Father Sherwood spun around. But he was too slow. He was flung across the room with the force of a gale. He crashed against the chairs and the study table. The cross now lay on the ground, out of reach.

> *"If Sherwood could*
> *He would cut wood*
> *But he is not good*
> *But he is not good"*

Russell recited the lines with a menacing grin on his face. The rhyme brought back painful memories to Sherwood. He had been given the task of chopping wood by Father Lynn and the axe had bounced back toward his face. He had instinctively put up his right hand as a defense to guard his face. The sharp axe had chopped off two of his fingers. Father Sherwood became the butt of jokes from the students behind his back. And this was the rhyme they used to recite and taunt him with. And one afternoon, Father Sherwood had walked past the dormitory, when he heard the rhyme and turned around to catch Russell Ainsworth reciting it. He had caught Russell by his ears and had taken him to Father Lynn's office where Russell had received a flurry of shots from a thin bamboo cane.

Father Sherwood dived and picked up the wooden cross from the floor and held it up. Russell put his hand out toward Father Sherwood who found himself being lifted up. A force began choking him. He was struggling to breathe. His feet were now dangling inches above the floor. Father Sherwood began to recite the Latin 'Prayer to Saint Michael'—a powerful prayer used during exorcism and to ward off evil spirits.

"Princeps gloriosissime caelestis militiae, sancte Michael Archangele, defende nos in proelio adversus principes et potestates, adversus mundi rectores tenebrarum harum, contra spiritalia nequitiae, in caelestibus.

Veni in auxilium hominum, quos Deus ad imaginem similitudinis suae fecit, et a tyrannide diaboli emit pretio magno."

[St. Michael the Archangel, illustrious leader of the heavenly army, defend us in the battle against principalities and powers, against the rulers of the world of darkness and the spirit of wickedness in high places.

Come to the rescue of mankind, whom God has made in His own image and likeness, and purchased from Satan's tyranny at so great a price.]

Russell screamed. Father Sherwood's cheeks started splitting open and forming a scar. The pain was unbearable, but Father Sherwood knew that he could not give in or give up. Through the pain, he continued to recite the prayer . . .

"Te custodem et patronum sancta veneratur Ecclesia . . ."

Russell kept screaming and then suddenly disappeared. Father Sherwood, free from the grasp of the spirit, crashed down on the floor in a heap. His body was drained of all energy. His face was a bloody mess. He crawled and then sat up on the floor, resting his back against the study table. He was glad that Father Lynn had taught him exorcism. He had never had the opportunity to use it . . . till today.

His old body ached and he groaned as he slowly lifted himself off the ground. He walked to bathroom and saw the scars on his face. He knew that he had had a narrow escape.

****

Suraj was aghast seeing Father Sherwood's face in the morning.

"Father, what happened to you?"

"Long story. Let's just say I had a visit from one of my old students who wanted his things back." Father Sherwood replied.

Father Sherwood got into his Fiat car, "I have some work to do. I will be back in a couple of hours."

He drove toward Spring Sidi Tea Garden. He parked the car outside the old British Graveyard. The man-in-charge was there to greet Father Sherwood. They both walked through the graveyard which had gravestones dating back to the 1800s. Father Sherwood had been here with Father Lynn on the day that Russell Ainsworth had been laid to rest. He knew where his grave was situated.

It was a gravestone with a cherub. The epitaph on the gravestone read:

"Here Lies Russell Ainsworth
(1947–1958)
Budded on Earth
To Bloom in Heaven"

Father Sherwood asked the man to dig a hole beside Russell's grave. When the hole was dug, Father Sherwood buried the tin biscuit box, said a prayer and sprinkled holy water on the site and asked the man to cover the hole.

Father Sherwood stood beside Russell's grave and said a prayer. He felt a sense of calm wash over him. He knew that Russell would not be visiting the school again.

Father Sherwood drove back to the school. The three of them were there to receive him. The children gasped on seeing his mutilated face.

"Aah! Don't worry. These are the scars of a battle. Rupert, your ordeal is over. Russell will not come to bother you anymore. Suraj, keep Rupert with you in your quarter. He needs to feel safe."

He addressed Bithika and Rupert, "Next week, I am arranging a trip for you two to spend the week traveling to Darjeeling and Kalimpong. I have spoken to Reverend Subba who has been kind enough to arrange your stay and sightseeing. Everybody is having a holiday—why should you two miss out on all the fun?"

Father Sherwood walked off.

"Father!" Rupert called after him. Father Sherwood turned around, "Yes Rupert?"

Rupert ran up to him and hugged him around his legs, "Thank you!"

Father Sherwood knelt down on his one knee and hugged Rupert back.

"It's all over. Russell has been laid to rest. You don't need to be scared anymore!

ABOUT THE AUTHOR

 Anirban Bhattacharyya is the producer and writer of *Fear Files*—one of the most successful horror-genre TV shows on Indian television.

He is the bestselling author of the true crime book *The Deadly Dozen: India's Most Notorious Serial Killers* and *India's Money Heist: The Chelembra Bank Robbery*. He has also written the bestselling bildungsroman memoir *The Hills Are Burning*.

He is the creator, producer, writer and director of *Savdhaan India*. He is also the producer of *Crime Patrol*.

Anirban Bhattacharyya was born in Calcutta and studied at Dr. Graham's Homes, Kalimpong. He did his B.A. (Eng) from St. Xavier's College, Calcutta. He did his M.A. (Mass Comm) in Film & Television from MCRC, New Delhi.

He has been the Head of Content at Channel [V] India. He has also been the Head of Non-fiction Content and Brand Solutions at The Walt Disney Company (India).

He is an award-winning Standup Comedian and a movie actor.

He is one of the few authors in the world who writes across various genres. He has published five books so far—three of them being bestsellers.

You can follow him at www.linktr.ee/anirbanb

Did you enjoy reading the book? If so, please visit the Goodreads and the Amazon page for the book and leave your reviews.

More from Fingerprint's Library

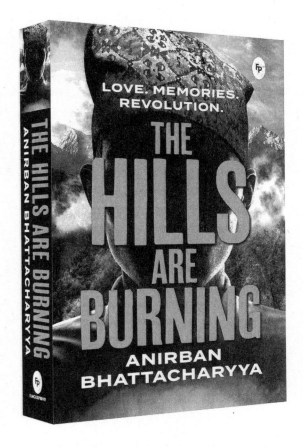